A PRINCE OF INDIA

A PRINCE OF INDIA

Laurence Clarke

Rupa & Co

A PRINCE OF INDIA

Laurence Clarke

Contents

1

Precautions

On an eventful afternoon in July, Dacent Smith, the Chief of Harland's Department in the India Office, summoned him, and fixed him through his monocle.

"I have a message for you, Harland, from the Under Secretary."

At the mention of the Under Secretary, Harland sat up straight in his chair. The Under Secretary was the permanent official who guided the destinies of the India Office, and, so far as the office was concerned, a personage vastly more portentous than the Secretary of State—a mere bird of passage, subject to the mood of the British elector.

"A very delicate situation has arisen, Harland," went on Dacent Smith. "Strickley—our Resident in Kathnagar—has an idea that his Maharajah is in some sort of danger, and he has been to the Under Secretary for advice. Strickley is growing old and is apt to be nervous and jumpy, but now-a-days we daren't run unnecessary risks"; he paused a moment. "Hence," he continued, "you are to get what may prove to be the chance of a lifetime!"

"Thank you," Harland answered promptly. "What is it that Strickley suspects?"

"He doesn't know himself," smiled Dacent Smith. Harland's eyes widened.

"He literally doesn't know," said Dacent Smith, blandly; "but you, Harland, are to see that nothing happens to the Maharajah of Kathnagar during this stay in England—you are to take care of him. Do you understand?"

Harland nodded.

"A sort of unobtrusive watchdog?" he questioned.

"Precisely," said Dacent Smith. "The Maharajah must now nothing of our precautions on his behalf. Personally," he continued, "I think Strickley may be wrong, but I have had enough experience of this Office to know that anything may happen where a Native Prince is concerned!"

He paused abruptly, then reached forward and grasped Harland cordially by the hand.

That was the end of the interview.

Thus it came that Harland, a few nights later, found himself loitering in a certain recess in company of marble statue of Phryne. The placid smoothness of his official existence as a clerk in the India Office had been broken at last—he had been entrusted with an extraordinary Mission, a mission quite outside the monotonous routine of the Office.

From his point of vantage in the depression in the wall he obtained an excellent view of the grand staircase of Galton House, of the extensive marble tessellated hall, of a multitude of dazzling white shoulders, of brilliant, coiffured hair, glowing uniforms and the soft black of dress coats.

The Duchess of Galton herself stood at the stairhead to receive her guests.

Harland moved from his retreat and launched himself upon the crowded floor of the hall. He was a clean-shaven man of twenty-eight, with a capacity for wearing clothes as they should be worn. He was black-haired, distinctly handsome, with a sun-tanned skin and direct blue eyes. Save for the servants and the detectives, who were no doubt discreetly watchful, he was the only person present with a purpose other than pleasure.

During his careful inspection of the guests he met several acquaintances, but it was not until eleven o'clock that the man he had been sent to seek appeared suddenly before his eyes.

The Duchess of Galton had forsaken the stairhead, and a few guests strolled upon the broad balcony, which branched therefrom to right and left. Here, leaning gracefully upon the onyx balustrade, Harland became aware of a slender, isolated figure surveying the crowd below. The figure was that of a man of thirty, wearing a jewelled turban—a man languorous of face, with a deep olive skin and burning Eastern eyes.

Harland knew in an instant that he was a potentate, that here was the man he had been sent to seek.

The Maharajah wore a tabard of lilac silk, lined with salmon-coloured satin; below the tabard appeared narrow stark white trousers, ending in the twinkling lacquer of a pair of Oxford shoes. Swathed about his neck were twelve rows of pearls of prodigious size, creamily lustrous even at that distance. From his right shoulder, crossing the tabard to the waist, ran a rope of smaller pearls as thick as a man's wrist, and visible upon his left hip was an ornate sword-hilt, a-quiver with jewels.

His Highness Sir Pirthi Rao Hadra Bahadur, K.C.S.I., Maharajah of Kathnagar, the most opulent of non-tributary Princes, was a young man of immense lineage, and was fifteenth in direct descent from Rao Hadra himself. Burning on his turban, and placed in the exact centre of the brow, was a stupendous rectangular emerald, bearing an invocation said to have been graven there by Rao Hadra's own hand. Edging the lurid green flame of the emerald ran a stream of brilliants, flashing back a thousand points of light to the crystal chandelier which hung above.

"Great Scott!" ejaculated Harland, with a quizzical light in his eyes, "and that's the man I've got to take care of!"

A light hand fell upon his shoulder.

"Well, did you recognise him?" asked a brisk voice.

Harland turned and caught the twinkle of Dacent Smith's monocle and the pink glow of his chubby face.

"It wasn't difficult to recognise him," smiled Harland.

They walked along the broad, voluptuously-carpeted balcony together, and Dacent Smith slipped an arm through Harland's.

"You can forgo your vigilance for half-an-hour," he said; "I want to introduce you to Strickley—our Resident in Kathnagar."

Dacent Smith and Sir Boris shook hands. Sir Boris Strickley, who had risen from a gilt-legged, tapestried chair, scrutinised Harland closely.

"Mr. Harland is gentleman specially selected by the Under Secretary," explained Dacent Smith, presenting Harland.

"I am glad the Under Secretary thought it worth while to

appoint someone," remarked Sir Boris. He paused a moment, and fingered the end of his clipped grey moustache. "It is a very delicate matter, Mr. Harland," he said, "requiring tact and—"

"That," broke in Dacent Smith, "is why Harland has been chosen for the work!"

Dacent Smith lingered a few minutes, then before he went away drew Harland aside.

"The Maharajah," he said, "is safe as long as he is at Galton House, but we must run no risks. See Strickley privately at the first opportunity, and learn anything you can from him."

He turned and went away with a complete absence of ceremony. Srickley put a lean hand to his moustache and ruminated, thoughtfully looking at the space Dacent Smith had a moment before occupied; then he turned his eyes towards Harland.

"I'm glad to meet you," he said: "I think the India Office has acted sensibly for once. We can't talk here," he said; "you must dine with me one day soon—" He moved across to a woman who was fanning herself upon a settee. She was probably fifty years of age, and had been extremely handsome.

"Charlotte," said Sir Boris, "this is Mr. Harland of the India Office."

Lady Strickley shook hands, smiled graciously and pointed to the vacant place at her side with her fan.

"Sit down," she said.

"You see," said Strickley slowly to his wife. "The Under Secretary thought there was something in what I said after all. He has detailed Mr. Harland—"

"That will do, Boris," said Lady Strickley, quietly touching her husband on the arm with her fan. "You can discuss matters when Mr. Harland gives us the pleasure of dining with us. Go and tell Anastasia I want her."

Harland instantly made up his mind that Lady Strickley was the dominant partner. Her unexpected amiability towards himself flattered and puzzled him a little.

Harland wondered who Anastasia might be, but a moment later he came to his feet as Sir Boris advanced towards them leading a tall, dark-haired girl.

"Anastasia," said Lady Strickly, "this is Mr. Harland of the India Office."

"How do you do?" said the girl.

Their eyes met. The eyes of Anastasia Strickley were beautifully shaped, were softly luminous, and shaded with long lashes.

A few minutes later Harland found himself deep in conversation with Anastasia Strickley, who possessed an exquisitely modulated voice and an animated temperamental type of beauty that appealed peculiarly to his imagination.

For a while the gorgeous vision of the Maharajah was obliterated from Harland's mind. He pulled himself together at length, and rose to his feet.

"I am very much afraid I must go," he explained to Anastasia; a pause followed. "I am not here entirely on pleasure," he continued.

"Indeed?" answered the girl. She looked up at him with a thoughtful, enquiring gaze.

Harland took his leave. Near the foot of the broad staircase he again saw the aigrette in the Maharaja's turban, and below it the satanic fire of his great emerald.

The Prince was in conversation with a squat, black-bearded

man, who wore the blue riband of the Garter across his shirt-front. Harland knew in a moment that the sombre-looking, bearded stranger was the Duke of Galton, and, as he moved nearer to obtain a close view of the Prince's features, he observed that the Maharajah's dark eyes wandered from the Duke, and appeared to sweep the staircase and the crowded floor searchingly. And all the while as he talked the Prince's slender, brown hand toyed unconsciously with the jewelled sword-hilt at his hip. Harland noticed that his face, upon close inspection, was handsome and delicately formed, that he carried himself with the air of a prince, that he was of the East, Eastern, in both carriage and appearance—and as he looked he became suddenly converted to Strickley's idea. Any thing might be possible where this Eastern potentate was concerned. As this thought slipped into his mind, his eyes travelled upwards, and he became aware of Sir Boris Stickley, who was descending the broad, blue-carpeted staircase with his wife and daughter. Anastasia, slender, beautiful, and graceful, held Harland's gaze; she was descending with her head slightly inclined towards her mother, who talked vivaciously. The girl listened with parted lips and a smile on her face.

Suddenly as Harland stood there he noticed that the Maharajah of Kathnagar had become tense with interest, that the expression of his face had altered, and that the presence of the Duke had slipped completely from his consciousness. His softly brilliant dark eyes were raised to Anastasia as she descended towards him; he made a swift move forward and ascended two steps.

Lady Strickley saw the movement; the smile faded from her face, her eyes darkened with displeasure, her handsome lips closed tightly.

2

Carter Takes a Hand

When Harland called upon him three nights after the reception at Galton House, he found his Chief busy at his desk correcting proofs of a report.

"Well," he said, "what news?"

Harland briefly narrated the result of his investigations. He had spent two days in keeping an unobtrusive watch upon the Maharajah, and as a result had satisfied himself that Sir Boris Strickley was right in his suspicion. There was no doubt of the fact that certain persons made a practice of following the Maharajah wherever he went. The chief of these persons, Harland had discovered, was a man who occupied rooms in Half Moon Street.

"What do you know of this man?" interjected Dacent Smith.

Harland took a strip of paper from his pocket.

"He is known at his apartments as 'Doctor Sanquo,' and is believed to be an American. He frequents the most expensive hotels, and appears to have unlimited money."

"You think the Maharajah is quite unaware that he is being shadowed?"

"Quite," answered Harland.

"I suppose you have formed no opinion as to what is in the wind—or why this man is following him?" asked Dacent Smith with a casual air.

Harland shook his head.

As he detailed the incidents of the past two days he noticed a marked change take place in Dacent Smith's manner. His Chief's casual air left him, and he showed himself distinctly uneasy and disturbed.

"You say," he said, "that the Maharajah is always accompanied by Krishna Coomar, his private secretary?"

"Always," answered Harland.

"Do you think Krishna Coomar is loyal to his master?"

"I agree with Sir Boris Strickley on that points," said Harland; "I think he is absolutely loyal to the Maharajah."

Dacent Smith rose from his chair and paced the floor with his hands behind his back.

"Look here, Harland," he said, after a minute's silence, "we'll have Krishna Coomar here to-night, and see what he knows."

He sat down abruptly and wrote a short letter, which he dispatched to Krishna Coomar at Galton House.

An hour later the Maharajah's secretary himself stepped quietly into Dacent Smith's small drawing-room. Harland was still there, seated in a deep armchair on one side of the fire, and Dacent Smith occupied a similar chair at the other; clouds of Turkish cigarette smoke filmed the air.

Krishna Coomar, with a polite smile upon his dark-skinned

face, stepped into the room. He was a cheery-looking, plump-faced man, with a coffee-coloured complexion and twinkling brown eyes. He wore spectacles with heavy gold rims, and Harland noticed particularly that his eyes were timid and plaintive in expression.

Dacent Smith introduced Harland, and Krishna Coomar, putting his plump brown hand into Harland's, bowed again and smiled.

"I am sorry to drag you out so suddenly at this hour of the night," said Dacent Smith.

Krishna Coomar remarked that it was of no importance. He was aware of Dacent Smith's position at the India Office, and if he could be of use in any way he hoped that Dacent Smith would permit him to offer his poor services. There was a moment's silence, during which Dacent Smith stared thoughtfully into Krishna Commar's face.

"Well," he said, "I want to ask you some rather peculiar questions."—Krishna Coomar bowed.—"You have been with the Maharajah for many years?"

"I have been with His Highness all his life," answered Krishna Coomar, with an air of dignity. "I was his teacher when His Highness was a small child. Since he has returned from Oxford he has honoured me with the appointment of private secretary."

"I believe," broke in Dacent Smith, "His Highness is very fond of you."

"He treats me as though I were his friend rather than his servant," answered Krishna Coomar, with quiet pride.

"My question is this," went on Dacent Smith. "During the past few months have you noticed that certain persons are following His Highness?"

Krishna Coomar's bright intelligent eyes turned towards Dacent Smith; then he rose abruptly from his chair.

"Yes," he answered, I have noticed it. Until this last week or two I thought it was my imagination, but since we have been in London I am sure that there are persons spying upon His Highness."

"Is one of these persons an exceptionally tall man with aquiline features?"

Krishna Coomar nodded.

"Can you give any reason why this man should wish to shadow the Maharajah?" questioned Smith.

Krishna Coomar stared thoughtfully before him for a full minute, then raised his head.

"There may be many reasons," he said.

There was silence for a minute. Harland, who had been closely regarding the dark coffee-coloured face, saw that the man was deeply disturbed. Krishna Coomar was of the clearly, timid type of native, and it was obvious to Harland that his devotion to the Maharajah amounted almost to fanaticism.

"Mr. Harland here," explained Dacent Smith, "has also noticed that the Maharajah is being spied upon. He has undertaken the delicate duty of watching the Prince on behalf of my department. I wonder," he went on courteously, "if we could ask your good offices in the matter?"

"My life is at the disposal of anything that may be done to secure His Highness's peace of mind and safety," answered Krishna Coomar, solemnly.

When at length Krishna Coomar had departed, with an assurance from Dacent Smith that everything should be done for the protection of the Maharajah, Harland also rose to go.

"Keep a close watch upon your Dr. Sanquo, of Half Moon Street," said Dacent Smith. "and remember that you have the whole strength of the Department behind you."

Three nights later Harland received a telephone message from Dacent Smith, and in the space of half-an-hour again presented himself on the threshold of his Chief's drawing-room.

Dacent Smith was engaged in animated conversation with a young man who was a stranger to Harland.

"Harland," said Dacent Smith affably, "you've heard of Carter?"

The man seated in the chair at the other side of the hearth rose. He was tall and handsome, with long lashed dark eyes and a brown complexion. As Harland gripped his hand, he felt instinctively that he was in the presence of a man of exceptional vigour and mental activity.

"I'm pleased to meet you," said Carter, smiling, and showing a row of strong white teeth.

"Carter belongs to the Secret Service Department," interpolated Dacent Smith, briskly. "In his opinion some attempt may be made to molest the Maharajah when he moves from Galton House. I have tried to persuade the Prince to return to India, but for some reason he is obstinate about it and won't go. He insists on staying in London for the present, and has taken a suite of rooms at the Golden Pavilion Hotel in the Strand. Now, Mr. Harland, you and Mr. Carter are to work together in the matter. You must both move to the Golden Pavilion Hotel. You must keep an unobtrusive watch over the Prince. Remember that in a sense he is the guest of the Government—it's up to you both to see that no accident happens to him."

3

The Golden Pavilion

"That's our man!" observed Harland, in a low voice. "Do you mean the tall fellow in the opera hat and the white muffler?"

"Yes."

Carter and Harland were seated together in the luxurious *foyer* of the Golden Pavilion Hotel in the Strand.

To describe the Golden Pavilion Hotel is to describe dream—the dream of Hypolyte Dufour—realised in brick and stone. Hypolyte had raised his dazzling white building, tier after tier of French windows, in a perfect, unrivalled position on the Thames Embankment; more over, Hypolyte, Prince of Hotel Proprietors, had lavished money on his Golden Pavilion as an Eastern monarch might lavish money on the palace of his heart's desire. The hotel, indeed, was a palace in everything but name; it was the most comfortable hotel in Europe, the most select and the most expensive. Two tall masts dominated the Golden Pavilion, one at the east, one at the west end of the building, and from these the French and English flags were flung daily to the breeze. Only occasionally, when some important foreign potentate was staying in the hotel, would the French flag disappear, to be replaced for awhile by the particular emblem of the monarch whom Hypolyte Dufour desired to honour.

The Maharajah of Kathnagar, disregarding broad hint conveyed to him from the India Office had decided to continue his stay in London. The Golden Pavilion suited his needs admirably, and, when Krishna Coomar had informed Hypolyte Dufour that His Highness intended to stay there for several weeks, the Prince moved into what is known as the Royal suite; whereupon Carter and Harland, acting under Dacent Smith's instructions, promptly took rooms on the same second floor.

"That's Dr. Sanquo without a doubt!" said Harland.

Carter rose and crossed the broad carpeted floor. A minute later he stood within a few yards of the circling glass door which gave entrance to the hotel.

The man pointed out to him by Harland had moved to the Bureau, and had been awarded a key. Carter, hovering some distance away, eyed the stranger closely and with deep curiosity. He noticed that Dr. Sanquo was a man of distinct force of personality, the manner in which he demanded his key, his air of distinction, his complete *savoir faire,* impressed Carter, who had never seen him before. When he turned from the Bureau, and Carter obtained a full view of his face, he noticed that the Doctor was lean, that his cheekbones were exceptionally high, and that his eyes were long and narrow. His dark cheeks were clean shaven, and his intensely black hair was smooth and glossy.

Carter watched him as he strolled across the *foyer* and

disappeared intot he interior of the hotel; then he returned to Harland.

"Well," asked Harland, "what do you think of him?"

"If that is Sanquo," answered Carter, dropping into the seat beside Harland, "he is no more an American than I am!"

"What do you make him out to be?"

"Eurasian," answered Carter. "I should like to see his finger nails."

Harland sat up abruptly.

"Eurasian?" he repeated.

There was silence for a few minutes, during which each man pursued his own train of thought.

"Come along," said Carter, abruptly, "we'll see if Hypolyte Dufour knows anything about him!" Harland rose from the purple-seated lounge.

They passed together to Hypolyte Dufour's little glass-panelled door. Carter knocked, and a moment later they were within the sacred precincts of Hypolyte's private den, a diminutive room, the walls of which were plastered with signed photographs of distinguished guests, who appreciated both Hypolyte and the supreme comforts of his hotel.

Hypolyte himself was an active, quick-eyed little Alsatian, who cultivated an Imperial, and wore a silk-faced frock coat and pointed patent boots. His age was fifty, and he had made a fortune in a period of eight years. Recognising Carter, he held out his plump, smooth hand.

"Charmed to see you, Mr. Carter," he said.

Hypolyte was one of the few persons in London who were aware of Carter's occupation.

"This is my friend, Mr. Harland," explained Carter.

A minute later, when Hypolyte had persuaded them to be seated, and had offered corpulent and opulent-looking cigarettes with the Khedival insignia upon them, Carter remarked: "I am after information as usual, Monsieur Dufour!"

Hypolyte bowed.

"These are most excellent cigarettes," remarked Carter, to fill in the pause.

"They are without parallel," assented Hypolyte; "the box was presented to me by the Khedive's secretary on His Highness's departure from here a month ago. This information, Mr. Carter?"

"Concerns one Dr. Sanquo, who arrived here to-night, but had evidently registered his rooms in advance."

"Dr. Sanquo?" repeated Hypolyte, and shook his head slowly. The name conveyed nothing to him. He rose, and crossing to the narrow mantelshelf, spoke into his private telephone. When communication had been established with the bureau, he demanded particulars, with the curt authority of an autocrat in his own dominions. A minute later, with the receiver still at his ear, he glanced at Carter.

"Dr. Sanquo," he said, "has not been here before. This is his first visit to the Golden Pavilion—and he is accompanied by a young friend, a Hindoo. Dr. Sanquo's valet is either a Hindoo or an Arab. This is the extent of our information."

There was silence for a minute; Hypolyte replaced the receiver on its hook.

"Where are Dr. Sanquo's rooms?" asked Carter.

"The second floor," answered Hypolyte, "one hundred and eighty-one, two, and three."

Carter glanced quickly and significantly at Harland, then spoke again to Hypolyte:

"The Maharaja of Kathnagar's rooms," he said, "are on the same floor—and only three away from Dr. Sanquo's."

Hypolyte nodded.

"Between Dr. Sanquo's rooms and the Maharajah's is a small suite vacant at present." A slight shade of anxiety had flitted across Hypolyte's good-natured face. "Monsieur Carter," he said, with an air of diffidence, "I trust you don't anticipate that anything unpleasant is about to occur—"

"Monsieur Dufour," remarked Carter, after a moment's thought, "you are discretion itself! The fact of the matter is that the India Office has merely detailed Mr. Harland and myself to watch over the Maharajah while he is in your hotel—a mere matter of precaution!"

A few minutes later, when Hypolyte's cigarettes had been consumed, and Hypolyte's fears partly allayed, Carter and Harland bade him adieu and strollled back again to the *foyer.*

"Why," asked Harland, as they went, "should an American doctor chance to have a Hindoo friend and a Hindoo valet?"

"The significant things," observed Carter, quickly, "is that Dr. Sanquo has engaged rooms as near as possible to those of the Maharajah!"

They discussed the situation for a few minutes, and at the end of that time a dark, portly form halted before them.

"I beg your pardon, gentlemen," said a voice in liquid Eastern tones.

Krishna Coomar, the Maharajah's middle-aged secretary, who had evidently been searching for them, exhibited a certain perturbation, and his fingers toyed nervously with a button of his frock coat.

"I thought it well to tell you," he said to Carter, "that the person who has been following His Highness has to-day taken rooms in the hotel—on the same floor."

"Thank you. Mr. Coomar," observed Carter; "but we are already aware of the fact, and shall take every precaution!"

"Thank you, gentlemen"; an expression of relief came into Coomar's dark eyes. "If I could persuade His Highness to return to India," he added, in low, thoughtful tone.

"Why does he insist on staying in London?" asked Carter.

A picture of Miss Strickley's beautiful eyes floated into Harland's vision; he thought he could guess why the Maharajah dallied in London. But Krishna Coomar shook his head, and displayed the palms of his hands helplessly.

"It is impossible to say," he murmured.

4

Disaster

Two nights laterHarland dined with Sir Boris Strickley, and
was presented for the first time to the Maharajah of
Kathnagar.

In the days that had elapsed since Dr. Sanquo's arrival at the
Golden Pavilion Hotel, a strict watch had been kept on the
Doctor's movements. Harland, who was enjoying his freedom
from office routine, had grown dexterous in the art of watching
unobtrusively over the safety of the Maharajah. He had watched
so discreetly that he was quite sure the Maharajah was unaware
of his existence.

The dinner at the Strickleys' took place at eight o'clock, and
when Harland arrived at the house in Bryanstone Square, he
found Sir Boris and Anastasia Strickely in the drawing-room. The
spell that Anastasia had cast over him at Galton House a week ago
still continued. She was certainly a most exquisite-looking girl;
the white gown she wore suited her admirably. She appeared
frankly pleased to meet Harland again, and greeted him cordially.

In that first moment after meeting her, he was inclined to think that he had exaggerated the significance of that scene upon the broad stairway of Galton House. He told himself that it was quite natural for an Eastern Prince to be attracted by a young girl of Anastasia's beauty, but it was quite unlikely that she would be attracted in return. The frank friendliness of her greeting towards himself encouraged him to remove the Maharajah mentally from the sphere of action. He began secretly to speculate upon the possibilities of a *tête-à-tête* with Anastasia Strickley. And at that moment a servant threw open the door and announced:

"His Highness the Maharajah!"

Sir Boris moved across the room to receive his guest. In the same moment Harland noticed that the colour had ascended to Anastasia's cheeks, that her eyes were lowered, that she had turned partly away. Harland's idea that the Prince was nothing to Anastasia Strickley vanished in a flash. He felt a poignant stab of disappointment that was almost jealousy. Then the voice of Sir Boris fell upon his ears—Sir Boris was presenting him to the Maharajah.

His first words to Harland came as a surprise.

"I am happy to make your acquaintance, Mr. Harland;" a quizzical look came into his eyes. "In England," he went on, "where there is so little sun, it pleases me to find that I still have my shadow!"

He smiled pleasantly, and Harland liked him on the instant. Nevertheless he felt more than little piqued to think that his tremendous efforts at concealment had availed him nothing. He realised something which Carter, or any other man versed in espionage, could have told him at once—that it is impossible to shadow an intelligent man for any length of time without being observed.

Harland had watched the greeting between Anastasia and the Prince, and save for the colour that mounted to Anastasia's cheeks, there had been nothing to indicate that a secret lay between them. Yet in Harland's mind there was no doubt of it. During dinner the Prince talked with light animation. His eyes appeared to linger upon the face of Anastasia, but he seldom addressed a direct remark to her, or she to him. Lady Strickley, magnificently handsome, in a determined matronly fashion, did a great deal of talking. Lady Strickley's attitude towards the Maharajah was outwardly everything that could be commended. But Harland, listening keenly, felt that he detected a hard ring in the matron's voice whenever it was necessary for her to speak to the Prince.

After dinner, when Harland followed Sir Boris and the Prince towards the drawing-room, an idea suddenly flashed into his mind. If the Maharajah were wide awake enough to know that he was being beneficently shadowed by Harland, surely he was aware of the attentions of Dr. Sanquo. What effect had that knowledge on his mind?—Was he afraid? Was he merely careless or indifferent? The Eastern mind is a dark mystery to the European.

What did it all portend? Why did the India Office not boldly acquaint the Maharajah of Sanquo's espionage in his own interests and demand his immediate return to his own country?

Then he recalled that the Maharajah of Kathnagar was an independent ruler, not even subject of British law. The idea that this slender young man in evening clothes who preceded him towards Sir Boris's drawing-room was an autocrat ruler of two million souls, and that this ruler was, as it were, in his safe keeping, appealed keenly to Harland's imagination.

A servant held open the door of the drawing-room, and the Prince entered the apartment. Anastasia, who was seated at the piano, wheeled on her stool, and Lady Strickley rose from her chair at the fireside.

"Your Mr. Coomar has not arrived, Prince," said Lady Strickley.

"Not arrived?" repeated the Maharajah. He glanced at the clock. "It is five minutes past nine," he added. There was surprise in his tone.

"Is he as punctual, as all that?" asked Lady Strickley.

"He is never late," returned the Maharajah emphatically.

During the rubber of bridge that followed, the Maharajah explained again that he had permitted Krishna Coomar to visit a friend that evening, but he was to come on to the Strickleys' at nine o'clock.

Harland, who was watching his face, noticed that as the minutes passed, and Krishna Coomar failed to appear, the Maharajah's interest in the cards waned.

At eleven o'clock a servant entered and announced the Prince's car. The Maharajah rose slowly, and with due ceremony bade adieu to Lady Strickley and Anastasia—Harland noticed a distinct prolongation of the hand-clasp between the Prince and Miss Strickley.

In the hall below the Prince's native valet was waiting to help his master with his overcoat and muffler. The Prince enquired if he knew the reason of Krishna Coomar's absence, but the man was without any information.

"Good-bye," called Sir Boris from the doorstep.

The Prince hurried across the pavement and stepped into his waiting Limousine. Harland, who had been invited to accompany him, followed; the door closed, and the car glided away.

There was silence for a minute, then Harland ventured a question:

"Your Highness is disturbed?"

"Yes. Coomar has never in his life been late."

"It is possible," speculated Harland, "that Mr. Coomar may have been unavoidably detained."

"That is the only explanation possible," answered the Prince quietly.

A few minutes later, as the Prince and Harland passed through the circling glass doors of the Golden Pavilion, they found the great *foyer* crowded with brilliantly-gowned women and men in evening dress. The Maharajah, accompanied by Harland, went immediately to the Bureau, and asked if Krishna Coomar were in the hotel.

"Mr. Coomar, sir? I'll enquire."

The clerk made enquiry by telephone, and was informed at length by Jones, the white-gloved, be-medalled commissionaire who guarded the circling exterior of the glass door, that Mr. Coomar had left the hotel about eight o'clock that evening, and had driven away in a taxicab—he had not yet returned.

"Thank you," said the Prince.

He glanced at Harland, then took out his watch. It was half-past eleven. They moved away from the Bureau together.

"He may have left a note or some word of explanation with my valet," said the Prince. "I will go upstairs and make enquiries."

"In the meantime," said Harland, "I will make further enquiries here."

The Prince bowed and went away. Harland saw him threading his way swiftly through the brilliant, animated crowd. He then began a search of the *foyer*; he was looking for Carter who had remained in the hotel to keep Dr. Sanquo under observation.

A quarter of an hour passed, during which Harland made enquiries and a thorough search of the public rooms of the hotel. But there was no sign of Carter or Dr. Sanquo; Krishna Coomar had also not returned.

It was now a quarter to twelve, and Harland took a position immediately by the revolving door of the hotel. He had waited there perhaps ten minutes when he chanced to glance over his shoulder. In the distance, at the far end of the *foyer*, he saw the Maharajah, who was evidently looking for him. At the same moment the circulating glass door swung round and a hand was laid on his shoulder.

Carter stood before him. He was wearing an opera hat and a long overcoat, his brows were contracted, and there was an ominous light in his handsome brown eyes.

"I'm glad you've come," said Harland, quickly; "Krishna Coomar, the Maharajah's secretary, left the hotel at eight o'clock, and hasn't been seen since. The Prince's more than uneasy about it—he thinks something may have happened to him."

"Something *has* happened to him," said Carter under his breath.

5

Hostilities

"**M**r. Harland," called the Prince, speaking as he advanced towards them.

"Leave the situation to me," said Carter under his breath to Harland.

"There was no note from Krishna Coomar in my room," said the Prince. He glanced across the hall at the great clock over the fireplace.

"Mr. Carter," he explained, after Harland had hurriedly presented Carter, "my secretary is missing! He was to have called for me at Sir Boris Strickley's house at nine o'clock. He has never failed me, and he is not now in his room—"

"I should like to suggest," said Carter, "that your Highness will not bother about the matter to-night. Mr. Harland and I will make every possible enquiry."

A few moments later the Prince, who had been somewhat reassured by Carter's words, retired to his room.

"Come upstairs with me," said Carter.

Harland followed him along the interminable, thickly-carpeted corridor on the second floor. Carter drew a key from his pocket and opened the door of his room; he carefully closed it behind him, and turned on the lights.

"Harland," he said, "Krishna Coomar is dead."

Harland's eyes widened in consternation and horror, but even then it came upon him that the news was not altogether unexpected. Until that moment he had been hovering on the verge of mysteries, now he felt that he was suddenly plunged deep into the vortex.

"How did it happen, Carter?" he asked in a low voice, and breaking a long pause.

"This is what happened," said Carter. "While you were at dinner at the Strickleys', I kept a careful watch on Dr. Sanquo, who remained in the *foyer* for an hour after dinner smoking a cigar and drinking his coffee. At the end of an hour he rose and left the hotel. I was curious as to the object of his journey and followed him in a taxi. At a corner of a street in Bloomsbury, the Doctor alighted from his own vehicle, paid the driver and dismissed him. I told my man to follow him slowly and at a distance. A few minutes later Sanquo entered, without ringing, 118, Gordon Street, a tall, gloomy-looking house with dingy windows, and an 'apartment to let' ticket on the ground-floor window.

"I alighted from my taxi and watched the house. For half-an-hour I strolled up and down on the pavement at the far side of the road. Then a singular thing happened, which I have not yet been able to explain. The front door of the house began to open slowly—so slowly that it scarcely appeared to move. It was only by the gradual widening of the stream of light from within

that I was made aware that the door was actually opening—
apparently of its own volition. A second later I discovered the
reason of the phenomenon. Dr. Sanquo was standing in the hall
behind the door and was drawing it towards him. When an
aperture wide enough to permit his egress existed, he stepped
out lightly, glanced about to see that he was unobserved, then
noiselessly closed the door behind him."

"He was merely escaping from the house," interjected
Harland.

Carter shook his head.

"Something a little more subtle than that," he said; "for the
moment the door was closed behind him, he turned and rang
the bell of the house. A minute later the door opened again, and
I saw a maid-servant in the aperture.

"The Doctor raised his hat—evidently asked her a question.

"The girl shook her head, waited politely until the Doctor
had descended the steps to the street, and then closed the door.
At first I thought of following the Doctor, who had walked
leisurely away; then it occurred to me to make a few enquiries
of my own at Number 118. In letting Sanquo go I remembered
that the Prince was safe with you at Strickley's house.

"I crossed the street and rang the bell, having waited until
Sanquo had turned the corner and disappeared. I waited a
minute, and was about to ring again when approaching footsteps
within reached my ears. Suddenly the footsteps halted, and a
loud scream rang through the house. I heard a woman's voice
calling, the sound of running footsteps from above; the next
instant the house door was flung open, and a servant came
hurtling out and collided with me where I stood on the top step.

"'Police!' she said in a hoarse whisper, 'Police!'

"A second later she was flying along the pavement with her white apron fluttering out behind her. I waited at the open door until she returned with a policeman. In the excitement the girl took no notice of me, and the policeman appeared to believe that I had a right to be there. In any case I remained unnoticed in the excitement, and followed the girl and the constable up the dingy staircase. On the first landing I saw a fat, breathless, red-faced woman, evidently the landlady of the house. Her eyes were wide with fright, and as the policeman advanced heavily, she pointed to a half-open door.

"'He's in there!' she said, 'I don't know who he is—I've never seen him before!'

"The policeman pushed open the door of the room. I followed and looked over his shoulder. Then the reason of Sanquo's secret visit there was made plain to me, for lying full length on a horsehair sofa was the body of a stout man in a tightly buttoned frock coat. Even before I saw his face I had guessed the truth—the body was that of Krishna Coomar. He was lying on his back with his head twisted curiously to one side; his skin was leaden in hue, and his gold-rimmed spectacles were still upon his closed eyes."

"My God!" ejaculated Harland in a low voice. "You mean that Sanquo has murdered him?"

"His neck was broken," went on Carter, "but there was no outward sign to show how it happened. The landlady found the body on the first-floor landing of the upper staircase. Of course at the inquest it will be assumed that Krishna Coomar fell downstairs and broke his neck."

"I suppose," said Harland, "that there is no doubt that Sanquo did it?"

"None at all in my mind!" answered Carter, "but I doubt if we can prove it. He evidently lured Krishna Coomar to the house with the intention of doing away with him. The whole thing was planned with diabolical cleverness. The poor fellow went there thinking he was going to meet an old friend; Sanquo slipped into the house afterwards and killed him!"

Harland rose and began pacing the floor anxiously.

"We must keep Sanquo away from the Maharajah!"

"He must be laid by the heels at once!" replied Carter. "I'll place the facts before Dacent Smith, and see what I can do the very first thing in the morning!"

Harland slept badly that night. The swift and merciless destruction of Krishna Coomar had put an entirely different complexion on the work he had to do. Who Dr. Sanquo was, what was the real history of the man, what was his mission, was a matter for busy speculation in Harland's mind. The fact that he had thought it worth while to risk the removal of Krishna Coomar proved that whatever his designs upon the Maharajah might be, they were planned upon large and utterly ruthless lines.

6

A Slender Stranger

The gorgeous dining-room of the Golden Pavilion Hotel was occupied by three or four hundred guests. Carter had not returned since the morning, and Harland, left to watch Sanquo, felt his nerves strung to a high state of tension.

Carter had departed from the hotel early with the intention of acquainting Dacent Smith of the death of Krishna Coomar, and he had requested Harland to keep a close watch on Sanquo. Of course it would be difficult to make the authorities act; some excuse would have to be discovered for arresting Sanquo. At any moment a couple of quiet-looking men might enter the dining-room of the Golden Pavilion Hotel and place themselves at Dr. Sanquo's table, or perhaps even now, Harland was not the only one who was engaged in secretly watching over the Doctor's movements. Harland had managed to secure a seat only two tables away from the Doctor, who dined alone. He noticed that Sanquo ate with excellent appetite—also that he wore his clothes with distinction—also that his smooth, black hair shone as if it had been lacquered—and that his complexion, when without a hat, appeared more sallow than he had at first imagined. Harland, as he ate his meal, occasionally heard Sanquo give an order to the waiter. On these occasions he noticed that he Doctor's voice was peremptory; he spoke in the tones of one to whom authority is habitual. There was none of the air of deprecation and suavity characteristic of Eastern nations.

The Doctor had laid down his knife and fork, and was leaning back in his chair. He sat motionless, and his eyes fixed themselves on Harland with a hard, inimical gaze.

He followed Sanquo into the *foyer* when the meal was concluded, and Sanquo again looked at him.

"He knows I'm watching him," said Harland to himself the second time he caught the Doctor's gaze.

Dr. Sanquo, after staring him out of countenance, both in the dining-room and in the *foyer*, took his coat and hat from the cloak room, submitted himself to the circling glass door, and disappeared from the hotel, and therefore temporarily from the scene of Harland's operations. It was no part of Harland's duty to follow the Doctor round London.

Harland wondered why Carter had not yet returned, went upstairs and along the corridor to the Maharajah's apartment. The Maharajah had that morning been informed of Krishna Coomar's death, and had remained in his rooms during the day. He had, however, sent a message to Harland that he would be pleased to receive him after dinner. At that hour of the night the upper floors of the Golden Pavilion were almost totally deserted, and as Harland moved along the empty corridor he saw in the far distance a dark figure approaching silently over the thick carpet.

A moment later, as the man drew nearer, Harland felt his senses grow suddenly alert with amazement—for a second he doubted the evidence of his eyes. During the space of a minute he could have sworn that the man advancing towards him, the man within five yards of him was the Maharajah himself! The stranger was slender, as the Maharajah was slender, he wore a long black coat, he was without a hat, and his handsome Eastern eyes rested for a moment on Harland as they passed within a yard of each other; but there was no light of recognition in their liquid depths. Apparently something in the fixity of Harland's gaze disconcerted the man, for he suddenly lowered his eyes. They were alone together in the endless dimly-lighted corridor, and as the distance between them widened, Harland felt himself suddenly seized with curiosity and suspicion.

The extraordinary resemblance of face between the man who had just passed him and the Maharajah of Kathnagar struck him as bizarre and unaccountable.

7

The Great Coup

A minute later, when Harland knocked at the Maharajah's door, and was admitted, he found the Prince seated at a writing table near the window of his drawing-room overlooking the Thames. He was habited in dress clothes that bore the unmistakable impress of Savile Row. Harland, who had come to condole with him on the death of Krishna Coomar, uttered conventional phrases.

"It is very kind of you," said the Prince, "to offer me your condolences."

The Prince took from his inner pocket a gold cigarette case opened it, and extended it towards him. Harland thanked him and declined the offered cigarette. Long afterwards, in a strangely different environment, Harland was again to recognise that cigarette case.

"It was an accident, Mr. Harland—this death of Krishna Coomar?"

His words were in the form of a question, and conveyed

themselves to Harland's ears with a strange intensity. He felt uncomfortable—the Prince's eyes were fixed upon his with a determined scrutiny.

"At the inquest this afternoon, your Highness," he said evasively, "the verdict was one of accidental death."

"Thank you," answered the Prince, and became silent. "I shall never know how faithful a servant he was to me," he resumed at length in a deep contemplative voice. He was silent a minute, and Harland rose.

"Can I do anything for your Highness to-night?" he asked.

He was endervouring to discover if the Prince intended to remain in his room for the rest of the evening; if so, no harm could come to him.

"Nothing," answered the Prince. "It is very kind of you to trouble yourself so deeply on my account."

"I thought if your Highness were going out to-night you might wish me to come with you."

The Prince glanced at the clock and, thanking Harland again, said that he intended to retire early.

A few moments later, when Harland had left the room, the Maharajah, seated in the gilt-legged armchair at the fireside, consumed a succession of the famous Khedival cigarettes—he had graciously accepted a box from Hypolyte Dufour. Many minutes later the feverish tinkle of the telephone bell on a little table at the far side of the room awoke the Prince from his reverie.

Again he glanced at the clock, and, with the swift light-footed movements that characterised him, crossed the room.

"Well?" he called into the receiver of the telephone.

"Is that His Highness?"

"Yes."

"How are you this evening, 'Rao'?"

The habitual gravity of the Prince's face departed, his eyes lit up with at smile of pleasure.

"I am very well, Anastasia, and you?"

"Yes, very well," answered Anastasia. "Are you alone?"

The Prince paused for a second, then responded gallantly, "in thought I am with you."

"And I with you," came the answer. "Listen."

There followed a pause, during which the Prince, with one hand resting on the top of the table, bent over with his ear to the receiver.

"And I you, Anastasia—with my heart I love you," he said at length.

Again he listened.

"If you are sure that your mother will not return, I will come at once; I shall be with you in fifteen minutes." Then he hung up the receiver and rang a silver bell.

When the tall Pathan had brought the hat and coat he required, and had helped him into the coat, the Prince turned and looked quietly into the man's impassive face. It was his intention, he said, to be absent from the hotel for an hour; he wished to leave unobserved, and desired his servant to conduct him out of the building the back way. The Pathan expressed no astonishment, and a few minutes later the Prince found himself descending the bare, narrow service stairs, attended by his valet. The man led him down what appeared to be interminable flights of uncarpeted stone steps, and at length issued into an asphalt-paved yard. At the door of a gate in a high wall the Prince dismissed his servant. A walk of fifty yards or so enabled him to emerge upon the pavement of the Embankment. He held up his stick, and a taxicab halted.

"Bryanstone Square," said the Prince, giving the number. He stepped into the vehicle, and sank back in the corner of the seat.

"You will please wait," he said in his sauvely authoritative manner, when he alighted from the taxi at the door of Sir Boris Strickley's house.

"Very good, sir."

Ten minutes elapsed, then a quarter of an hour, and the gay little instrument attached to the taxi continued its life work of earning money for its master. At the moment when the chauffeur lit his second cigarette he was conscious of a slight rocking movement or tension. His sub-consciousness informed him that someone had stepped softly into his vehicle—his consciousness, however, repudiated the idea, and he continued to smoke. He was not an observant man under any circumstances, and in any case he was scarcely likely to notice that a taxicab had followed him from the Embankment, and had halted scarcely twenty yards behind him. This vehicle had now disappeared, and its fare, a man in a long dark coat, had also disappeared.

The chauffeur's hunched contemplation came to an end when the door of Sir Boris Strickley's house opened, and the Maharajah appeared on the threshold. The prince descended the steps and crossed the pavement.

"Drive me to the Thames Embankment," he said, "and drop me where you took me up."

The driver made a convulsive upward movement of his left hand, and jerked his head down a little to one side. This was the nearest approach he ever made to civility. The Maharajah drew open the door of the vehicle and stepped into its dark interior.

As he relapsed upon the seat, his heart leapt suddenly, some woollen substance was pressed heavily over his mouth, a grip of iron closed about his slender throat. The pressure and tension upon his neck were beyond endurance. Another second, and he would have been struggling frantically for his life, bereft almost of reason by the rapidity and violence of the attack upon him. Then the grip of iron relaxed, and an even voice whispered in his ear, "If you cry out or utter a sound—" the long hard fingers enclosing the Prince's throat tightened a little, and the Maharajah understood.

He was lacking neither in courage nor in a certain agile strength but the man beside him possessed three times his muscular force. Moreover he possessed, the faculty of conveying by his touch that the Maharajah's life was in deadly peril, and that the least attempt to call aloud would end in destruction.

In the moments that followed, as the taxi rolled smoothly through the London streets, and the lights gliding past the windows illuminated the interior of the cab, the Maharajah's eyes sought the features of his assailant.

He saw a dark-skinned man without a hat, a man with smooth back hair, high cheekbones, and long narrow eyes. The man's hand was upon his throat, and his hard relentless gaze was fixed intently upon the Prince's dark, sensitive eyes.

Dr. Sanquo was engaged upon the "coup" of his life. He could have broken the Prince across his knee with ease. What his intentions were was not fully known until long afterwards, but his daring capture of the Maharajah was without doubt the culminating moment of a long and deeply-planned conspiracy.

Before the taxi reached the Embankment, the Maharajah realised that for the moment his position was hopeless—there was nothing for it but to submit to superior force. The taxi stopped at the identical spot whereon the Prince had entered it. For a vague, unaccountable fraction of time he believed that episode of the past ten minutes had been nothing more than a fantastical, terror-inspiring dream. Then he drew himself stealthily together. A swift resolution to slip from Sanquo's grip and to leap to the pavement animated him. But again hope left him—a new figure darkened the window of the taxi—the door opened and a man stepped silently inside.

"Tell him where to go," said Sanquo in a low voice.

The man who had entered put out his head and gave an order to the driver. A moment later the dazzling façade of the hotel vanished from the Maharajah's sight. The taxicab had started again, and rolling rapidly eastward.

8

Harland Thinks of Something

Harland, having said good-night to the Maharajah, retired to his own room with an easy conscience. The Prince evidently intended to spend the remainder of the evening in his own apartments. Nevertheless, Harland as a precaution made two separate journeys along the corridor past the Prince's suite and down into the *foyer* of the hotel. Here on each occasion he scrutinised the brilliant crowd, but there was no sign of Dr. Sanquo, neither did the Prince descend to the public rooms again that evening.

At eleven o'clock Harland felt himself justified in retiring to his room. The evening was warm, and he threw open the French window and stood for a minute looking out over the gleaming black waters of the Thames. As the minutes passed Carter's long absence began to strike him as significant. He found himself growing uneasy. In the distance Big Ben chimed the half-hour. Then the strange, murmurous silence of a great city at night descended upon his room again. He felt himself growing tense and nervous, so much so that when a rapid knock smote the panels of his door, he started and leapt round as though someone had attacked him from behind.

Then he laughed at his fears, crossed the soft carpet, and opened the door.

On the threshold stood Carter, wearing a grey, soft felt hat and a long grey overcoat. His face was haggard and white. The rather quizzical smiling look that usually dwelt in his eyes had departed, his lips were pressed together in a thin line.

Without a word of greeting he stepped forward into the room and closed the door behind him.

"Harland, old man," he said, "you must brace yourself for a piece of bad news!"

"What news?" asked Harland.

"They've got the Maharajah!"

"Got him!" Harland stared stupidly.

Carter nodded.

"Unless our luck turns, old chap, both your official career and mine have come to an abrupt end. It's the devil's own luck, but we've been outmanœuvred—somebody's been making rings round us!"

"Got the Maharaja!" repeated Harland in a voice that was hoarse and almost inaudible. "You don't mean—"

"The Prince has been kidnapped," retorted Carter in sharp staccato tones, "vanished off the face of the earth! This fellow Sanquo has made rings round us."

"It's impossible!" said Harland.

"The whole thing is one of those deep Eastern mysteries that no European can fathom! There's no doubt about it! The Maharajah was in the hotel and was safe enough a couple of hours ago. After that he made a secret visit to Anastasia Strickley—"

"Anastasia Strickley."

"Yes," answered Carter. "It seems that when the Maharajah left Strickley's house Miss Strickley watched him get into a taxi which was waiting at the door. She was concealed behind the curtains of a room on the first floor, and she avers that as the taxi drove away she saw the Prince in its interior struggling with another man. Her first instinct was to warn Dacent Smith by telephone. I happened to be with Dacent Smith at the time. I have never seen a man so utterly flattened out. You and I haven't much to lose, but his whole lifework—"

"Go on!" said Harland, breathlessly.

"Well, of course," went on Carter "I came here like the wind, and went to the Prince's rooms. His Pathan servant was there, but the Prince had vanished. The man told me that he led his master out of the hotel by the servants' staircase; then conducted him through the hotel yard, and out on to the Embankment. This was a little after nine o'clock. He saw the Prince hail a taxicab. He evidently went straight to Miss Strickley, and must have been followed there by Sanquo. For I have found a chambermaid who saw Sanquo on the servants' staircase a few minutes after the Prince passed down it."

Carter suddenly raised his head and came abruptly to his feet.

"Now Harland, we must act! We have just one chance in a thousand before Scotland Yard begins to meddle in the affair. The first thing we must do," he said as he crossed the room and took his hat from Harland's bed, "is to learn all we can about Sanquo's movements. If he is in the hotel now, we must never lose sight of him. I suggest that you stay here and watch for Sanquo. In the meantime I will go to Miss Strickley and see if I can find out anything more from her. We've got to find the Maharajah at any cost! Of course, we may have difficulty in tracing him. Heaven only knows what's behind all this—what that fiend means to do with him."

Harland was already pulling on his overcoat and had grabbed his hat. Together they went out of the room and along the corridor. As they passed Sanquo's suite of rooms, Carter bent to the level of the keyhole.

"Either out or gone to bed," he said to Harland in a low voice.

They ran downstairs together and into the *foyer* of the hotel. There was no sign of Sanquo.

Outside the circulating glass door stood the giant commissionaire. He smiled and nodded to Carter.

"Jones," remarked Carter in a casual voice, "do you know if Dr. Sanquo is in the hotel?"

"No, sir, he hasn't come back this evening."

For a minute Carter and Harland talked aside. Then Harland made a suggestion that had been occupying his thoughts.

Carter was silent for a moment, staring thoughtfully before him. Suddenly he looked at Harland with a quick gleam of excitement in his eyes.

"That's a great idea!" he said, "but don't let Sanquo find you there!"

Then he stepped into a waiting taxi and glided noiselessly away over the rubber pavement of the courtyard.

9

A Louis Quinze Bed

Half-an-hour later Harland put his great idea into execution. He inserted a master key, obtained from Hypolyte Dufour, in the lock of Sanquo's door, and opened it with infinite caution.

The room was empty.

On the ceiling two ladders of light from the uptilted Venetian blinds reflected the Embankment arc lamps. Something in the air—an odour unfamiliar and Eastern—greeted his nostrils. He closed the door behind him, and in the darkness crossed to the next room of Sanquo's suite. Again he cautiously opened the door, and again found darkness, and that heavy odour which reminded him of the East. Both rooms were empty. The shutters of the second room were also closed. Harland therefore had only to assure himself that the third room was empty before carrying out the object of his mission—the search for papers that might lead to knowledge of the Maharajah's whereabouts.

The apartment he was in and the one he had passed through were arranged as sitting-rooms, therefore the one he was about to enter was Sanquo's sleeping chamber. He paused a moment and listened. The intense silence was broken by the muffled sounds of life upon the Embankment. He advanced at length towards the third door, opened it softly, then recoiled a step or two.

The room before him was in darkness, but a light glowed in the attached bathroom.

As in Harland's room, the bathroom door fitted to this chamber was panelled with panes of ground glass.

It was behind this glass that the light was burning. Harland paused and, hearing no sound, moved softly forward, the rich carpet deadening his footfalls. He saw that the bathroom door was an inch ajar, and standing aside so that the beam of light issuing into the room would not reveal his presence, he extended his neck and peered through the aperture.

In the bathroom a tall, almost black-skinned Asiatic, wearing trousers and a pink undervest, was drying his hands on a towel. With each movement his massive bare arms gleamed in the electric light. The man wore a sparse beard and his face was in shadow, but Harland could see the whites of his eyes as he glanced about him, drying his hands the while, oblivious of the man who watched him through the door.

Harland moved back a pace. He was conscious of a distinct feeling of chagrin and disappointment. The fellow in the bathroom was evidently one of Sanquo's servants, and his presence there completely frustrated the object of Harland's visit. For a minute he remained motionless watching the man through the aperture of the door, and thinking rapidly. The feasibility of locking the fellow in the bathroom and leaving him there came and went in his mind. But bathroom keys are invariably to be found on the inside, not on the outside of the door. Then a swift resolution took Harland—after all, there was urgency in the cause of his visit there. His entire future and Carter's future depended on the recovery of the Maharajah.

He had entered that room armed, and prepared if need be to make a capture of Sanquo himself. A little display of force could do no harm. Harland took a step forward and put a hand on his hip-pocket. At that moment he heard a faint noise behind him, the quiet of the room was broken by a low voice calling "Hajiz! Hajiz! Hajiz!"

The voice was urgent and issued from the darkness within a foot of Harland's ear. Forgetting the man in the bathroom and the potentialities of those powerful dark arms, Harland flung round.

Instantly something lithe and snake-like enveloped his elbows—he felt at violent jerk, then the truth broke in upon him—he was being swathed in ropes.

In the darkness an unseen enemy had flung a rope about him. The dexterity of the movement amazed him. He leapt forward towards the door with all his strength and crashed to the carpet. He tried to rise, the hempen rope enveloping his legs brought him to the floor again. He was full of fight, and using both feet together, struck upwards with all his power. "Hajiz," who had issued from the bathroom, bent low and came at him; Harland's Oxford shoes crashed against his jaw and sent him leaping backwards with a yell. The man ran to the window nursing his chin in his hands and howling savagely. Harland was still kicking like a madman when a gentle pink glow suffused the room.

Light gave place to darkness.

Dr. Sanquo stood at the lamp switch looking at his victim. He was glancing from the corners of his eyes, but he was entirely unperturbed; even his peculiar, glossy, blue-black hair was unruffled; there was a gleam in his eyes and a triumphant smile played about his lips.

During the struggle not a word had been said. Harland had saved his breath for the fray, and Sanquo, except to bring Hajiz to his aid, had said nothing.

Hajiz was still bending double in the window, laying tender exploratory fingers on his injured jaw. Sanquo motioned him to lift Harland to the bed, but Harland drew himself up to kick, and Hajiz recoiled into his corner.

Harland's eyes turned to Sanquo. If looks could have slain the Doctor, he would have died in that instant. For a moment Harland's humiliation amounted almost to a frenzy; it seemed impossible that the Doctor could have overwhelmed him in this facile and easy manner. He had assured Carter that it did not matter if the Doctor caught him in those rooms. Like a fool he had underestimated Sanquo's daring and resource. He cursed himself for his fatuity.

The man who had ruthlessly slain Krishna Coomar and had spirited away the Maharajah of Kathnagar was clearly an exceptional personality. As he looked at Sanquo now he noticed the harsh angle of his jaw and the triumphant expression in his pitiless eyes. He wondered what was the history of the man, what lay behind these amazing actions of his. Clearly he was no ordinary criminal; money did not enter into his calculations, and yet in no other way could Harland account for the kidnapping of one of the richest Princes of India. Perhaps, however, Carter was right after all, and Dr. Sanquo was the head of some sinister Eastern conspiracy. Some mysterious Oriental movement may have decreed that the Maharajah of Kathnagar should be abducted, and Dr. Sanquo had been deputed to carry out the work. One thing comforted him as he lay there upon the floor striving to realise what had happened to him—Sanquo did not yet know that he and Carter were aware of the Prince's capture.

He determined, whatever happened to himself, not to mention the matter to Sanquo.

Dr. Sanquo came across the room and looked down fixedly at his overthrown and humiliated enemy. His voice was quite pleasant and easy as he spoke: "We have things to settle, you and I. You have been hanging on my heels for some time."

"Untie these ropes, or it will be the worse for you!" called Harland. They were the first words he ever uttered to Sanquo.

"I have been expecting you any day for the last week," retorted Sanquo, smoothly; "now you are here we won't beat about the bush—"

But Harland was not listening. He had discovered that his right hand still retained a certain freedom of movement. A latitude of six inches was at his command, and he was stealthily bringing his hand towards his Colt revolver when Sanquo flung himself upon him, turned him on his face, and disarmed him.

"Now, Hajiz," he called, "take him under the arms!"

His voice was sharp, rasping, and compelling. The dark and powerful Hajiz came forward, making a detour to avoid Harland's legs. A minute later Santquo and his servant were lashing Harland to the bed. They laid him on the billowy counterpane and passed slender hempen ropes completely round the bed, precluding even the faintest possibility of escape.

Harland's Oxford shoes were against the panelling of the Louis XV bedstead: he was able to move his head and his feet—that was all; otherwise he was helpless and completely at the mercy of the men who looked down upon him. Harland kicked and resisted with all his strength.

"Damn you!" he called out in helpless fury when he was finally conquered.

Then the fatuousness of anything he could say in his present helpless condition struck him, and he stared sullenly at the ceiling.

"I am a man of large interests," said Sanquo, a minute later, standing at the bedside looking down at him. His tone was that of a business man discussing a business matter any day in an office. "Persons who intrude themselves into any affairs"—he stooped, and bending low over Harland looked into his face—"are liable to meet with accidents."

Harland was conscious that Sanquo was using his eyes to intimidate him, but despite the Doctor's advantage, Harland returned his gaze without flinching.

"If you think," observed Hrland, "that you can make away with me as you did Krishna Coomar you are mistaken!"

The words had scarcely left his lips when he felt that he had made an irretrievable mistake, for Sanquo stepped back with narrowing eyes.

"I know nothing of Krishna Coomar," he said.

But he was visibly disturbed, and the smooth suavity of his voice had disappeared; it was again harsh and rasping.

"Hajiz, wait in the outer room!" commanded Sanquo.

Hajiz paded obediently to the door and went out. He closed the door softly behind him.

Sanquo turned his chair a little, and leaning over the bed looked down into Harland's face. Harland read a purpose in the narrow scrutiny, but he was not a man to be easily intimidated.

"Assuming it to be true that I killed Krishna Coomar," said Sanquo, with perfect calm. "Possibly he was in my way—as you are in my way; you came here to-night to spy on me, and this is the result—you find yourself neatly laid by the heels."

The Doctor rose, placed his chair against the wall, and lit a cigarette.

"Isn't that true?" he asked, looking at Harland over the flame of the match.

"It is pretty obvious," said Harland from the bed. He was not afraid; perhaps the suddenness of events had dazed him a little. He was wondering when Carter would return. He had every confidence in Carter—he believed that if the Maharajah were in London, Carter would discover him. In the meantime it was an advantage that he and Sanquo should be engaged in this strange *tête-à-tête* together. Sanquo's presence there was a guarantee that at the moment he was not actually dangerous to the Prince's life.

The Doctor spoke again.

"You understand your position?"

"I understand perfectly your anxiety to escape the law," retorted Harland.

For some minutes there was silence; he wondered if Sanquo were at a loss what next to do.

"Krishna Coomar died—very suddenly."

"Very suddenly," remarked Harland. He understood the threat underlying the words. "I am not so friendless as Krishna Coomar," he continued, confidently.

Sanquo eyed him narrowly.

"Not so friendless?" he questioned, and paused a minute. "You mean that you have other friends who are interesting themselves in my affairs?"

"Several," returned Harland. Sanquo moved his head quickly.

"There are at least half-a-dozen people watching you in this hotel alone," continued Harland, driving home the thrust. "The fact that you have captured me does not in the least matter!" His eyes sought the Doctor's. He fancied his thrust had rather more than repaid the Doctor's hit.

To Harland's surprise Sanquo made no answer. He rose from his chair, however, and began to pace the floor slowly, with his head bent in thought.

Suddenly Sanquo halted, turned in a flash, and moved to the bedside.

"Six of you?" he enquired slowly.

"Yes," answered Harland recklessly.

Sanquo looked again at Harland—and paused a moment "In that case you won't be missed," he said.

"What do you mean?" asked Harland. Sudden misgivings, sudden doubts as to the wisdom of those fine thrusts of his went leaping through his thoughts. Horrible doubts began to creep assiduously at the back of his mind.

Sanquo bent and ran his fingers over the ropes binding Harland to the bed.

"You lie! You alone are spying upon me! You alone have invented this story of Krishna Coomar's death!" said the Doctor in a low, intense voice; "that is unfortunate for you."

He called Hajiz in Hindustani, spoke a few words to him, and the big dark fellow, evidently obeying instructions, advanced to the bed and helped his master to partially unbind Harland and bring him to a sitting position. His hands, previously lashed to his sides, were now bound at the wrists behind his back. Sanquo drew the cord tight, and Harland called forth all his fortitude to repress a cry of pain.

Suddenly the Doctor thrust him back on to the bed again. There was something ferocious in the action that startled Harland.

"Your family will have no unpleasant mystery to clear up," said Sanquo, sauvely; "you will merely fall from the balcony of your own room on this floor. It is so natural for a young man who has dined well to step on the balcony of his room for a breath of air—and it follows quite simply that he may overbalance and fall into the yard below, breaking his neck."

The Doctor's words had been delivered with an unction that was satanic. There was no doubt now of his intentions.

Harland's senses grew strangely clear; he speculated on the chances of a sudden call for aid, a wild dash—tied as he was—for the door.

Hajiz spoke in Hindustani, and Sanquo answered him. Harland swiftly reckoned the distance from his own window to the flagstones below. There was just one chance in a hundred, even if the worst came to the worst, that his neck might not be broken in the fall. With the wonderful buoyancy of youth his mind seized on and clung to that fragmentary desperate hope.

The Doctor was again eyeing closely, perhaps he detected that faint gleam of hope in Harland's mind; in any case the true Sanquo—the Eurasian—leapt into view. For a moment the implacable Eastern cruelty, the Eastern indifference to life, revealed itself through the thin veneer of civilization.

"I see that you are thinking that the fall may *not* break your neck?" He looked about the room, glanced at Hajiz, then said in a low voice. "That will be *arranged beforehand!*"

A shudder ran down Harland's spine; the horror of his position gripped him at last. He realised now that this thing had been coming upon him from the beginning, from the very moment he had entered that room!

For some minutes he stared hopelessly at the ceiling, he felt that his forehead was damp; but even in that moment his pride resented this involuntary betrayal of his feelings. Suddenly a fierce rage swept over him; he knew that he would willingly die a death of lingering torture if he could have just five minutes, only five minutes' freedom, to confront these two villains on his feet.

Sanquo took out his watch and stood at the bedside, looking at it much as a doctor looks at his watch in examining a patient's pulse. Harland's preternaturally clear senses fathomed his object. He was waiting for twelve o'clock, waiting for the lights in the dining-hall to be extinguished. It would not do to have the body of a murdered man flash past those shining windows, and fall with a crash into the yard below. What was the time? How long was there to wait? Harland bit his lips to prevent himself putting these questions to Sanquo. But the Doctor had seen his eyes on the watch.

"I'll tell you what time it is" he said; "there are exactly nine minutes to twelve."

Thank God! That was something. He knew now how long. Carter had evidently not returned. His thoughts, suddenly became obscured, a sensation of coma stole over him. Sanquo had turned away and was folding something at the table. Harland guessed, but paid not heed. A faint silver disc of light on the ceiling caught his vague and wandering eyes; his dreamy gaze followed it, as eyes without volition always gravitate to light. It was the size of a five-shilling piece, and doubtless reflected a stray light from the Embankment—yes—that was far away. Cabs tinkled by and motor horns hooted faintly, but only intensified the silence in this sinister room, with the impassive Hindoo leaning against the wall, the impassive man in evening clothes folding something at the table, the impassive figure bound hand and foot on the bed! ...

Harland made a mighty effort to pull himself together, and his mind began to leap here and there, seeking some loophole of escape. The minutes were creeping by. ... Sanquo might turn at any moment now. Harland closed his lips firmly ... At any moment the first busy-body of a clock might begin to strike ... He prayed that his courage might hold, then cursed himself for a coward in praying.

He pulled himself together and faced it.

"Roomal," that was the word. *"Roomal!"* Krishna Coomar had died by the *"Roomal."* The sinister handkerchief, the instrument of Thuggee, the trick of which had descended in India from generation to generation since the thirteenth century. ... He tried to recall things that he had heard of that terrible, swift form of strangulation. It was something with the thumbs. ... Sonquo's thumbs were brown thumbs—they were strong—excessively long thumbs. ... but it was the trick, something in the. ...

His mind relaxed again, and settled in the disc of dancing light on the ceiling. It came through the closed latticed shutters, and flashed and disappeared intermittently. No doubt the branch of a waving tree on the Embankment intercepted its rays. ... The little disc of light began to bob stupidly—and became still—and bobbed again. ...Gradually Harland came up, as a man rises from deep waters—as a man awakes from uneasy dreams. His senses began to order themselves, and concentrate upon the little point of light above him.

Suddenly he felt the blood leaping through his veins.

What was that? ... Of course the tension was telling on him ...This hallucination—this idea that there was a conscious rhythm in the movement of that five-shilling disc of light—was ridiculous. It was the mania of a drowning man who clutches at something even less helpful than a straw.

The light was still now.

He would be circumspect, and cool, and quite calm this time. He would begin again, and watch it from the beginning.

Dot—dash—dot! Dot—dash—dot! Dot—dash—dot!

F.F.F. The opening signal of the Morse code! The call of one operator to another. Then again:—H-A-R- What was that? The light flashed, disappeared, flashed again.

H-A-R-L-N-D.

"Harland, answer this!"

He stared—glanced at Sanquo and Hajiz. How could he answer? He was bound hand and foot—it was idiocy to make such a request.

Sanquo moved to the bedside at the very moment that Harland decided to call aloud—to risk everything in a last desperate shout for help.

"Carter—"

The world never left his lips, for Sanquo's brown, strong hand leapt upon his mouth.

"I was expecting that," said Sanquo, "but no one would hear you, my friend!"

A premature, distant clock began to strike the hour of twelve, and Harland, lying on the bed with Sanquo's hand pressed over his mouth, found his brain growing strangely clear. He had never been so near death as at that moment, yet precisely then—when at any instant Sanquo might slip a sinister handkerchief from his pocket—he found courage to kick the foot of the Louis XV bed loudly and rhythmically. The cool daring of sending this message, as it were, from the very jaws of death outwitted even the Doctor. Harland, tapping his Oxford shoes upon the polished wood of the bed, was able to spell out one word for help, when Sanquo turned swiftly, seized him round the waist, and whipped him off the bed to his feet.

10

Hypolyte's Adventure

"Is that Monsieur Dufour?"

"Yes, monsieur."

"This is Carter speaking."

"Yes?"

"I want your help on a confidential matter."

Hypolyte, who had received many confidences of late, threw out his chest; he almost bowed into the telephone receiver.

"My services are always at your request."

"It concerns my friend Harland," said Carter. "I expected to get back to the hotel hours ago, but most pressing circumstances have detained me."

"I understand," interjected Hypolyte, "you are unable to return!"

"I am unable to return to-night, and I am anxious about Harland. In pursuit of his duty to-night," went on Carter, "he was obliged to make-a search of certain rooms in your hotel—do you understand?"

"I am aware of that," responded Hypolyte, his intelligent brown eyes brightening with interest.

"Well," went on Carter, "they were dangerous rooms to search, and I want you to find out if he is safe. I have been ringing him up in the main office, and the clerk tells me he is not to be found in the hotel. He ought to have finished the work he had in hand hours ago—" There was a pause. Hypolyte drew himself up magnificently.

"I understand, Monsieur Carter, that you place your friend, his safety in my hands."

"Precisely," responded Carter. There was relief in his voice. "Who knows," he added a moment later, "that the Government some day may not see fit to reward you—"

"No, no, no," protested Hypolyte, "no rewards, no honours."

A latent instinct for martial action enabled him to slough the hotel proprietor, and become a soldier, a warrior, a sleuth-hound, in a period of less than five minutes. For it was scarcely five minutes later when Jones and Hawkins, his giant guardians of the circling door, stood respectfully before him. These two vast men bulked so largely in his little room that they entirely obliterated the end wall. Hypolyte danced before them like a marionette. Their slowness of comprehension maddened him. They were willing to do anything—they were capable of hairbreadth adventures, but they were slow, oh, so devastatingly, slow, in grasping the situation.

"Monsieur Harland, you understand," said Hypolyte for the tenth time, "has ventured into this suite of rooms—he has been in these rooms for hours—therefore he is a prisoner there! You understand this is a matter of the greatest delicacy and secrecy. We must discover whether Mr. Harland is safe or not!"

He opened a drawer in his desk and took out a black, flat, automatic pistol.

"Do you understand firearms?" he questioned with an upturned eye on Hawking's stolid face.

"Not automatics," said Hawkins.

"Do you?"

Jones shook his head.

"Very well," concluded Hypoyte; "you are large men, you can rely on your hands!" He slipped the pistol into his pocket. "Follow me!"

The two commissionaires followed sheepishly.

On the second floor, as they approached Sanquo's apartments, Hypolyte motioned them to remain in the distance; then he advanced, and with a conspiratorial air softly turned the handle of one door after the other of Sanquo's suite. All the doors were bolted from the inside; but there was a light in Sanquo's bedroom.

Hypolyte could hear a voice from within. He recognised Harland's voice. Harland was swearing—Hypolyte's quick Gallic apprehension visualised the whole scene behind that closed and bolted door. Harland was Sanquo's prisoner— mysterious and secret happenings were toward! If all Monsieur Carter said were true, it might be dangerous to attempt to force that bolted door—dangerous to Harland's life. ...

Suddenly Hypolyte thought of attempting to enter the room from the window overlooking the Thames. There were balconies to all the windows. A board laid from the balcony of an empty room next to Sanquo's suite would enable him and one of the men to crawl perilously to Sanquo's balcony itself. Then if the window was open, Harland would be rescued.

If five minutes Hypolyte had put his audacious plan into execution. A plank had been placed from one balcony to the other, and Hypolyte, on hands and knees, and wearing his frock coat, had crept stealthily over it, and with equal stealth had let himself down upon the balcony of Sanquo's bedroom. Then followed Jones—fourteen stone of muscle and brawn habited in a gorgeous royal-blue uniform. Jones's pluck was magnificently tested in that moment when he reached the centre of the plank, and the plank creaked ominously over the abyss.

"Mon Dieu," breathed Hypolyte to himself as he watched the giant commissionaire creep towards him, "these big English fellow are slow, but they are not afraid!"

Jones stepped down softly behind his master, and wiped his brow with the back of his hand.

"It is a great misfortune," whispered Hypolyte, "that the window is closed and the blinds drawn."

On hands and knees he crept forward and strove to peer through the upslanting Venetian blind. A strip of the ceiling illuminated by the pink shade of Sanquo's lamp was all that rewarded him.

He turned to Jones with an expression of despair on his face.

"Anything, anything may be happening," he whispered. "This is a most serious matter! If the window had been open, I could have leapt into the room, and all would have been well for poor Monsieur Harland. Now—mon Dieu! If I make a noise—"

Then it was that the one brilliant idea of Jones's life illuminated his brain.

"I should think, sir," he whispered, "a gentleman like Mr. Harland might know the Morse code."

"Morse code? What do you mean—Morse code?" whispered Hypolyte. He was in despair.

"If he knew the Morse code," went on Jones stolidly—thoughts having actually begun to percolate through his mind were not easy to check—"if he knew the Morse code, we might send a message through the blind there. Then somehow or other he might think of a way of answering it. You said he would be expecting Mr. Carter to come and rescue him. Well, if he is he'll be looking about, and he'll say to himself, 'There's Mr. Carter signalling to me.'"

Hypolyte, whose eyes had been fixed in stare on Jones's face, darkly illuminated by a distant arc light from the Embankment, suddenly understood.

"We must get a mirror," said Jones.

He made a motion towards the plank spanning the chasm between the two balconies; but Hypolyte was not sure that the plank could sustain that fourteen stone a second time, therefore he went along it himself.

And five minutes later Jones, who had been standing silent on Sanquo's balcony, trying to distinguish words in Sanquo's room, saw his master creep back again, breathless and triumphant.

Hypolyte thrust the torch and the small shaving mirror he had brought into Jones's hand.

"Quick—quick!" he whispered. "Tell him—tell Monsieur Harland that we are here, that Monsieur Dufour is here to save him! Monsieur Dufour is here to save you," he repeated in Jones's ear.

Jones was now kneeling on the lead floor of the balcony, with the mirror in his hand, and the electric torch shining upon its surface. Hypolyte knelt at his side with his fists clenched, his head on one side, his ears straining to catch the slightest sound.

"Are you telling him that?" he palpitated. "Have you given him my message?"

"No," said Jones stolidly. "I haven't managed to get the light on to the ceiling yet."

He went on stolidly with his work. Then he suddenly glanced at Hypolyte.

"It's all right sir; the light's on the ceiling now. If he looks up he'll see it."

Hypolyte watched in breathless excitement. The apparently aimless darkening and illumination of the mirror fascinated him.

"You've sent my message now?" he breathed.

"No," said Jones, "I've only been able to give him the opening signal, and to spell his name."

Suddenly Hypolyte flashed a hand out and grasped Jones by the wrist.

"Hark!" he gasped. "What 's that? That tapping. That noise! Listen!"

Jones was listening with all his ears. Suddenly he rose to his feet, and stared at the closed window.

"It's help, sir—he's signalling for help!"

"Help—mon Dieu—Help!" cried Hypolyte; and instantly went insane, or rather he gave that impression to Jones. For he emitted a shout that was something in the nature of a battle-cry and hurled his small trim figure at the closed window.

"All right, Monsieur Harland!" he cried at the top of his lungs. "All right! One minute—One minute!"

But the window did not give.

Then Jones, infected by the excitement of the moment,

absently, wafted his master aside with the back of his hand, and hurled his own great figure at the window-pane. There followed a rending of wood, a creak of iron, and a loud splintering of glass. Jones plunged again with all the weight of his mighty shoulders.

"Burst! Burst! Burst!" screamed Hypolyte in a delirium of excitement. Then Jones plunged again and window and Venetian blind shot inwards, Jones with it. For a minute the big fellow staggered forward into the room, then fell on his knees.

Like a tiger Hypolyte leapt in after him, with a pistol in his hand.

"Ah!" he shouted. "Ah!"

Then his eyes fell on Sanquo, and he covered him with the weapon. Leaning against the bed with his hands tied behind him was Harland, his face white and his lips set in a firm line. Beside him was Sanquo under cover of Hypolyte's pistol. Sanquo was calm—his long, narrow eyes looked down into Hypolyte's—he was striving to calculate whether he was really in a trap or not. Was the door behind him guarded?

Hypolyte was formulating a speech of conquest when Sanquo's hand moved slowly, then swiftly. The electric light was knocked from the table and extinguished, the Doctor ducked, bent double, and leapt towards the door of his inner room. As his bent figure flashed though the inner door, Hypolyte turned and fired. Two shots pursued the Doctor through the doorway. Hypolyte followed the shots, calling out, "Hawkins! Hawkins!"

Hawkins, who had been stationed in the corridor to guard against a retreat of this sort on the Doctor's part, was too late, for the Doctor leapt out of the door of his sitting-room and escaped down the service stairs of the hotel in a flash. In the matter of beating a retreat when the odds were against him Dr. Sanquo's talents were unique.

Hypolyte returned from his pursuit and breathlessly re-entered the Doctor's apartments. Jones had freed Harland from his bonds.

"He's escaped!" cried Hypolyte, bursting into the room. "He was not even wounded!"

"You couldn't get him?" Harland spoke, putting the question with a note of keen anxiety in his voice.

Hypolyte raised his hands.

"He slipped through my fingers like butter."

"I'm sorry for that," said Harland; "it's important we should get him."

Then he suddenly remembered the service Hypolyte had done him, and held out his hand.

"Thanks," he said. "You came just in time!"

"What was—" inquired Hypolyte, solicitously, "what was it Dr. Sanquo intended to do?"

"He intended to dislocate my neck first, then drop me from my own balcony to the pavement below," answered Harland, quietly.

"Mon Dieu!" cried Hypolyte. "What a fiend. And I missed him! In my excitement I fired too high. The bullets intended for this fiend are now lodged in the beautiful walls of the Golden Pavilion Hotel!"

He paused a moment, put his hand dramatically upon his heart, and looked at Harland. He and the man he had saved from death were face to face—it was a stupendous moment!

"Nevertheless," he said, "you, Monsieur Harland, are safe."

Harland rose to the occasion.

"I owe my life to you, Monsieur Dufour," he said.

Dufour glanced at the bemedalled Jones, who was still wondering why he had failed to grab Sanquo as the Doctor darted from the room.

"We must not forget Jones," Hypolyte.

Harland did not forget Jones. Jones that night was remembered to the extent of a five-pound note.

11

The Precipice

Harland awoke next morning with a start, and as he opened his eyes the events of the night before flashed again through his brain. He rose with a sense of dejection and oppression that was accentuated by the gloom of the day, and the fact that distant church bells were pealing lugubriously. He shaved himself in his little circular mirror, and a servant tapped at the door.

"Mr. Shooter Quilliam wishes to see me?"

"Yes, sir!" answered the man from the threshold. "He is in Monsieur Dufour's parlour, sir."

"I'll be down in five minutes."

The door closed, and Harland groaned at his reflection in the mirror.

Five minutes later he was making his way through the gloom of the corridor—even the Golden Pavilion Hotel is gloomy at this hour on a July Sunday morning—towards Hypolyte Dufour's little private room on the ground floor.

Hypolyte's parlour was fussy, like himself. It was a room next his private office, some fifteen feet square, and was congested with an amazing medley of Sèvres china.

There were three chairs in the room, one of which was occupied by a little china group of dancers. The other two were occupied respectively by the Right Honourable Shooter Quilliam, Chief Secretary for India, and Detective Snow, a large man with a black moustache who was amazingly guarded in his manner.

Leaning against the table itself was Hypolyte, wearing a frock coat and little pointed patent shoes. There was silence in the room as Harland made a gingerly progress forward.

"Ah, Mr. Harland!" said Hypolyte, extending a small hand.

They shook hands, and Hypolyte went softly out of the room.

Quilliam rose from his chair. He was a cumbrously-built man of thirty-seven, with a heavy, clean shaven face—a face that was truculent and masterful. His hair, which was thining a little at the top, was reddish-brown; his lips were full and petulant; and his small eyes, fixed on Harland's face, were hard and ruthless.

"You are Mr. Harland!"

The words shot from his lips like the crack of a whip.

"Yes."

"You understand," said Shooter Quilliam, in a voice of menace, that would have quelled a mob—"you understand the significance of what has happened?"

"Yes," Harland answered.

"The Maharajah of Kathnagar, whom you and Mr. Carter were detailed to guard, has been decoyed away—kidnapped!"

He jerked his head in the officer's direction.

"Wait outside," he said.

His words removed Snow from the chair, and wafted him outside the room as though an invisible force had lifted him. When the door had closed, he halted face to face with Harland.

"Do you know," he said, "that what has happened has the makings of a national calamity?"

By the making of a national calamity he meant that his own official life was in jeopardy. Harland felt utterly a fool. He could merely murmur an acquiescence.

"What are you going to do about it?"

Shooter Quilliam's deep voice rose from a growl to a squeak.

"If the Prince is alive, Carter will rescue him," answered Harland, with conviction.

Shooter Quilliam's eyes searched Harland's face.

"Alive!" he repeated. He hesitated. For a moment he appeared almost helpless.

"You haven't any ground for supposing—"

"I'm afraid so," answered Harland.

"My God!"

Until how Harland had made no defence, had offered no excuse; but Quilliam's attitude jarred his nerves.

"It's not my fault," he broke out suddenly. "Nor is it Carter's fault that the Maharajah has been kidnapped."

"Eh?"

Quilliam's voice was a shrill squeak.

"It's the fault of Scotland Yard and yourself," retorted Harland.

In uttering the words he was committing official suicide, and he knew it.

"My fault?"

Quilliam's voice had fallen to a whisper. He appeared to possess an extraordinary range of personal expression.

"Carter requested a week ago that this man, Dr. Sanquo, should be instantly apprehended. He pressed the matter upon you time after time—"

There was a pause for a minute. Shooter Quilliam's features relaxed.

"That's true," he admitted, "quite true! Well? Where is Carter now?"

"He is searching for the Maharajah; he began his search last night, after Monsieur Dufour, acting on his information, saved my life."

"Saved your life?"

"Sanquo was arranging to strangle me as he last week strangled Krishna Coomar, the Maharajah's secretary."

"The verdict in that case was accidental death."

"In my case it would have been the same!"

"Harland," said Shooter Quilliam, "I am on the edge of a precipice—and you are on the edge of a precipice—I am not sure that you are not over the precipice. We have one chance in a thousand of smoothing this matter over, and keeping it out of the papers. This fellow Sanquo—I am presuming that you and Carter are right in believing him to be the prime mover in the business—this fellow Sanquo must be put out of harm's way. We are going to forget that Sanquo escaped out of this hotel last night, through the inefficiency of Carter and yourself—" He paused a moment. "Remember, Harland, I have forgotten your failure, you have *carte blanche*—the whole power of the

Government is behind you. If you restore the Maharajah unharmed, you will be performing a national service."

His smile came again—he held out his hand.

"We are going to forget your mistake. Can I rely on you?"

"Yes," said Harland, fervently, "you can rely on me."

Shooter Quilliam laid a hand on his shoulder.

"There is only one thing I ask," he said. "If you and Carter do find the Maharajah, in the name of mercy persuade him to get back to Kathnagar without delay. We've done everything that diplomacy can do to get him to go, but nothing can move him!"

Harland was silent for a minute. He was not an acute diplomatist, but a spark of genius had quickened in him unexpectedly.

"I can suggest something," he said, "that will make the Prince return to India by the next boat."

Quilliam's eyes looked a sharp, doubtful interrogation.

"Send Sir Boris Strickley back to Kathnagar," said Harland.

Shooter Quilliam did not see point. He recalled that Sir Boris Strickley was fever-ridden, and past work.

"We think of removing Sir Boris," he said coldly.

"Send him back to Kathnagar with his wife—and daughter."

"Eh?"

Shooter Quilliam's squeaking interrogation parted his lips, but this time there was a quizzical light in his eyes.

"Daughter," repeated Harland.

"Oh!"

Quilliam laughed. Then, with a swift transition of mood for which he was remarkable, his face suddenly clouded.

"This position of suspense is intolerable!" he said. "The man Sanquo's history seems to be utterly unknown to the police."

"In my opinion," said Harland, "he is merely a unit in a vast Indian conspiracy."

"A seditious conspiracy?" questioned Quilliam, focussing all his attention on Harland's answer.

"A seditious conspiracy," answered Harland; "but I don't see what His Highness of Kathnagar has to do with it."

12

Harland Forgets His Manners

For a week following his great adventure Harland remained kicking his heels helplessly in the Golden Pavilion Hotel. Carter, the Maharajah and Sanquo had vanished utterly from the face of his world.

His anxiety on Carter's behalf grew steadily—it was strange that Carter, usually so effective, should fail to communicate with him.

Ten days passed, and complete dejection seized him.

Dr. Sanquo, as a master of villainy, towered in his mind as a colossal, a devastating figure. He himself had escaped from Sanquo's fingers by extraordinary good fortune. What of Carter and the Maharajah? That was a question he was always asking himself, and always failed to answer save with a shudder and a sensation of shrinking and dread.

Shooter Quilliam appeared to share his fears; he was incessantly telephoning—incessantly asking for news. Mentally Shooter Quilliam saw his own theatrical and superb ascent to eminence ending in cataclysmic disaster. His mind's eye was perpetually occupied with the flaring headlines that might any day scream out of the Opposition papers.

"Disappearance—Assassination of an Indian Prince in London. Famous Indian Maharajah. What is the Indian Office doing? Shooter Quiliam ..."

Dacent Smith, who bore the brunt of Shooter Quilliam in office hours was in despair.

One night, when Harland was miserably alone in the vast *salle à manger* of the Golden Pavilion, he saw advancing towards his table a figure that he knew. Dacent Smith was trotting towards him, his monocle a-twinkle, his smile in startling evidence. They shook hands—Harland wondered as to the meaning of that of that smile—and Smith imposed himself upon a chair produced for him by Hypolyte's silent genii.

"Is Carter found?" asked Harland, breathlessly.

"Please! Please!" implored Dacent Smith; "if you won't interrupt me, I'll begin at the beginning. Quilliam's been like a madman all the week; he wants you to do something. If you refuse, I shall be a cold corpse inside three days. It's impossible to live with Quilliam when he's in this state of mind."

"If you're going to tell me about Carter or the Prince," responded Harland, "I'll listen to you. I don't want to hear anything else."

"The Star of the Orient," said Dacent Smith casually, "leaves Tilbury Dock at nine o'clock to-morrow morning. Quilliam wants you to take passage in her to India!"

Harland stared in amazement, and protested that Center must be found first.

"You needn't worry about leave or anything else," evaded Dacent Smith; "all that will be arranged."

"Don't say *arranged,*" growled Harland. "I hate the word arranged! What abut Carter?"

"It's at Mr. Carter's request that you're going," answered Dacent Smith.

"Then he *is* safe," said Harland. "Why couldn't you say so?"

"If it is ever my good fortune to become Prime Minister," said Dacent Smith, "I intent to present Hypolyte Dufour's cook with the Order of Merit and a K.C.B. By the way, all your expenses will be paid out of the Secret Service Fund." He inspected the greve on toast.

He was determined not to return to the subject of Carter's disappearance or the reason for Harland's departure by the *Star of the Orient.* This pose of mystery amused Harland; he read it as a good omen. At any rate Carter was safe, and if it were Carter's wish that he should travel to India with the boat leaving in the morning, Carter was, no doubt, on board, and big things might be toward. He wondered what these big things might be, but Dacent Smith was mute on the subject.

To a man of Harland's austere habits a sudden journey of this kind presented no difficulties, and at the appointed time next morning he mounted the gangway of the *Star of the Orient,* and was directed to his cabin by an important-looking steward.

"Give me the passenger list," said Harland, as he unlocked his suit case. The steward dived into a side pocket and produced it. Harland seated himself on the washstand, and scanned the list of names; them then a head was thrust in through the cabin door, and a voice cried: "Hallo!"

Harland saw Carter's smiling face before him, and sprang to his feet.

"What a mystery-monger you are, Carter," he said, extending a cordial hand, which Carter gripped with equal cordiality. "And where is the Maharajah—"

Carter silenced him with a gesture.

"I've been busy, my boy, with dark and mysterious operations," said Carter, still with a broad smile of pleasure on his face. "I couldn't communicate with you direct. Did you accept Quilliam's offer?"

"You mean that the secret Service Fund would pay all expenses?" questioned Harland.

Carter nodded.

"*Carte blanche,*" he said; "spend what we like. And if we fail, the whole British Empire and Shooter Quilliam go up in a cloud of smoke!" He clapped Harland on the back in sheer gratification at meeting him again. "Come along to my cabin," he said; "there's more room there."

They went along the deck, and entered a sumptuous four-berthed cabin, where a slender man in a brown lounge suit was hanging clothes on a row of pegs in the far corner, and a steward was unstrapping Carter's luggage.

"Who's that?" asked Harland, in a low voice, nodding towards the man who was hanging clothes with his back towards them.

"We haven't decided on a name yet," answered Carter, laughing. "His real name's as long as my arm." He glanced at the steward. "You can go," he said.

The steward rose and went out, closing the door behind him. Carter moved softly across the cabin, and laid a light hand on the shoulder of the man in the corner.

"Your Highness," said Carter, "here is Mr. Harland."

"I am delighted to see you again," said the Maharajah of Kathnagar, turning and holding out his hand.

"Well, I'm damned!" gasped Harland, entirely forgetting his manners.

13

The Chief of Police

An air of complete good homour prevailed; Harland had recovered from his surprise, and three of them were impregnating the cabin with the odour of the Maharajah's cigarettes. Nothing had been explained; the mystery of the Maharajah's disappearance and the mystery of his discovery were still a mystery to Harland.

"Is there any news of Dr. Sanquo?" asked Harland.

"None whatever," remarked Carter. "The mandarins of Scotland Yard insist with an ardour that amounts to violence that he has escaped to India. The Indian Police, on the other hand, are determined that he has remained in London.

"In the meantime he is at large," broke in the Prince, in his quiet voice.

"And," added Harland, "for all we know, may be on this very ship. After what has happened, I would believe anything of him. Your Highness is travelling incognito?" he enquired, after a pause.

"At Mr. Carter's suggestion," answered the Prince; "the India Office appears to be anxious to wash its hands of me And as Mr. Carter represents the India Office, and as Mr. Carter has also saved my life—"

"Hardly that," broke in Carter modestly. "I believe you would have escaped even if I hadn't found you."

"Where did you find the Prince?" asked Harland, who had restrained his curiosity quite as long as was humanly possible.

"To be precise," smiled the Prince, "Mr. Carter found me on a mudbank at Gravesend.

"In the cabin a steam yacht," Carter amplified,.

"When I have explained, Mr. Harland will be able to judge for himself whether my life was in danger or not," said the Prince.

The Maharajah narrated his adventure in the taxicab, then went on: "The next thing after that," he said "was an ill-smelling little cabin on board a steam yacht on the Thames. I was pitched into the room in darkness, and the door was locked upon me. There were two portholes in the cabin, but the brass screws, were beyond my strength to turn, and the portholes were shrouded from the outside. Then I felt the throb of an engine; the vessel began to move. For two hours I occupied myself with wild speculation as to what would happen to me. Then something did happen—not to me, but to the vessel I was in. Suddenly the floorboards shivered beneath me, there was a heavy grinding sound, then a crash, and the engine stopped working.

"That accident, collision, or whatever it was," he interjected, "was a providential thing. It broke the propeller of the yacht, and she was obliged to lie up until a new one was provided.

"In the meantime," went on the Prince, "Mr. Carter had discovered where I was."

"How did you do that?" asked Harland, turning to Carter.

"I learned from Miss Strickley what make of taxi it was. Fortunately for me it was not one of the better-known makes; but there are four hundred of its sort on the London streets, and a hundred and fifty ply the Westminster district. I went through them all systematically, one after the other, until I came to the man who had driven from the back of the Pavilion Hotel to Bryanstone Square. The same man drove Sanquo and his confederates to the yacht. After that it was easy. The police helped me to get the Maharajah away. Fortunately Sanquo's two confederates were captured, but Sanquo himself escaped."

It was not until the vessel arrived at Bombay, and the Chief of Police came aboard, that further light was thrown upon Sanquo's doings.

The Chief of Police, a tall, keen-featured mad of fifty, stepped into Carter's cabin the moment the ship reached the port.

"Mr. Carter?" he asked.

"Yes," answered Carter.

The Chief of Police introduced himself. In his inner pocket was a wallet stuffed with cables from the India Office. He drew them forth without preliminary.

"These," he said, "are bearing upon the case of the man Sanquo."

"Have you got him?" asked Carter, abruptly.

"No," answered the Chief of Police.

"Can you tell us anything about him?"

"Everything."

Two minutes later Carter and Harland—the Prince was not present—were seated on the bunks in the cabin, with the door open. The Chief of Police had made himself comfortable on the corner of the washstand.

"Your Dr. Sanquo is a son of Gunara Tukaji," began the Chief of Police, "and Gunara Tukaji is known from one end of Asia to the other. If you ask me," he went on, "she is just about the most dangerous individual in the Indian Empire. She comes of a Burmese family, and married Addison, a Scottish cotton merchant, in the seventies. In those days she was said to possess striking beauty; but she was always a schemer, always stirring up strife wherever she went. During the past ten years we have discovered traces of her in every seditious outbreak in India. Her son, Sanquo, was educated in England. Two years ago, in Bombay, he set up a seditious printing press. He is evidently following his mother's footsteps."

"What do you think his game was in England?" asked Carter.

"I haven't a notion," said the Chief of Police "unless he hoped to make converts to the 'India for the Indians' cause. England is full of cranks of every sort.

"As far as I can make out," went on the Chief of Police, "there seems to be some connection with the Maharajah of Kathnagar, but as the Maharajah has returned to India, and is safe in Kathnagar, there can be no danger there."

"Returned to Kathnagar!" The words issued from Carter's and Harland's lips simultaneously.

There was a long silence.

"You say the Maharajah of Kathnagar has returned to Kathnagar?" asked Carter, in a quite, deep voice.

"He returned to Kathnagar ten or twelve days ago," answered the Chief of Police, a little puzzled by their attitude.

Carter glanced at Harland, and in a flash the face of the man whose striking resemblance to the Maharajah had aroused his suspicious in the Golden Pavilion Hotel arose in his mind.

"Are you sure," he asked, suddenly, "that the man who has returned to Kathnagar is really the Maharajah?"

"I see no reason for doubting it," said the Chief of Police, still more puzzled by the question.

"Great Scott!" ejaculated Carter. He too, suddenly understood.

Carter and Harland stared at each other comprehendingly, much to the bewilderment of the Chief of Police.

"I am afraid, gentlemen," he said, "there is a mystery here that is beyond me."

Carter turned towards him politely. "I hope you'll excuse us," he said. "As a matter of fact, what you have said has taken our breath away. We were prepared for surprises when you came aboard, but not for this! This completely outshines and overtops anything we had foreseen. It explains something that has been a mystery until this moment. You say the Maharajah is in Kathnagar?"

"Certainly."

"As a matter of fact," said Carter, slowly and quietly, "His Highness the Maharajah of Kathnagar, is aboard this boat, and has travelled from England with us under an assumed name!"

The Chief of Police rose from his washstand and eyed Carter closely and keenly. Then he shook his head slowly.

"There is a mistake somewhere," he said. "I can prove that the Maharajah was in Kathnagar two days ago."

Carter glanced significantly at Harland, and Harland slipped quietly out of the cabin.

Two minutes later he returned, and stood aside to permit a slender, agile figure in a white duck suit to enter the cabin.

The Chief of Police, who had drawn out his sheaf of cables, and was flicking them over, seeking something, glanced up and uttered an exclamation.

He stared from Carter to the Maharajah and back again.

"How do you do?" said the Maharajah of Kathnagar, extending his hand.

14

Captain Taylor Appears

The next evening the much-enlightened Chief of Police stepped into the Maharajah's sitting-room in Booth's Hotel, Bombay.

"Well," he said, with cheerful, incisiveness, "we have managed to get to the bottom of the mystery at last."

Harland and the Maharajah were reclining in deep wicker chairs, and Carter, who had followed the Chief of Police into the room flung his hat on the table.

"As I expected," said the Chief of Police "Gunara Tukaji is at the bottom of the business. Her brain conceived the plot that has been carried out against your Highness. Gunara Tukaji perceived that if she could secure a powerful ruling prince who was disloyal to England, her campaign of sedition would receive enormous impetus. No such prince was to be found, and she hit upon the daring idea of substituting a puppet ruler in your Highness's place."

"Yes, yes!" broke in the Maharajah. There was a note of impatience in his voice; his fingers twitched a little.

"When a man was found who sufficiently resembled your Highness," went on the Chief of Police, "Sanquo followed you to London, taking the man who was to impersonate your Highness with him. You see the idea, gentlemen it is as clear as daylight; it was so much easier to substitute this fellow for His Highness while he was travelling in Europe, than when His Highness is in India, surrounded by scores of people who know him."

The prince rose from his chair and walked to the wide-open window.

"Can you," he asked, in a low, smooth voice, "suggest who this man can be who is impersonating myself?"

A brief silence followed. Through Harland's mind there again flitted a memory of the Native he had met in the corridor of the Golden Pavilion Hotel, the man who struck him by his remarkable likeness to the Maharajah.

"The man who is impersonating your Highness in Kathnagar," said the Chief of Police to the Maharajah, "is a mere tool of Sanquo's and Sanquo's mother."

"You say the man strongly resembles me?" broke in the prince.

"In appearance—yes."

"What is his name?"

"He is known by the adopted name of Amoola Khan."

"What is his history?"

"He is you Highness's half-brother."

The Prince looked at him quickly.

"I have never heard of his existence."

"His existence was not acknowledged," explained the chief of Police, "He is a person of no importance."

❖

That night, when the Prince had gone to his room, Carter and Harland sat together over final cigars.

A singular taciturnity seemed to have settled on them both. The superb effrontery and daring of Sanquo and his mother had at first left Harland merely astounded and incredible. Then it crept into his mind that there was something rather fine in this tremendous effort to stir strife and discord among several hundred millions of people. He wondered if the mysterious Gunara Tukaji were conscious of the magnitude of the work she had engaged upon. Sedition is not a pretty word, and the British Government is inclined to do something more drastic than to merely tap the fingers of persons detected in its practice. Truly, Gunara Tukaji was as great in her way as she was dangerous. No one but a woman of greatness could have conceived the idea of seizing an entire Indian principality.

Harland—contemplating his own tobacco smoke and Carter's ruminating, intensely absorbed figure—recalled the Maharajah's attitude of that afternoon. His slender figure had stiffened in its chair as the news of what had happened became clear in his brain; the suave Prince of India, who had made so languid and superb a figure as he leaned over the silver-and-onyx balustrade of Galton House, showed for the flashing instant of time in his naked Eastern fury; for a moment his dark, handsome face had been truly malignant. Five minutes later he had been again master of himself, and had inquired quietly, but with ominous smoothness, for the full details of then man who had usurped his position.

Then the case of Sanquo occupied Harland's mind. He and Carter were agreed that there was no doubt Sanquo was also at Kathnagar, lurking in the shadow of that bogus prince of his. If Sanquo were there, doubtless Sanquo's mother was there also!

What a coup—what an epoch-making coup he and Carter would achieve it they could gather in the whole crew of them at one sweep!

The Maharajah's demand, when the full case had been laid before him, was that the Indian authorities should instantly take public action in the matter. Carter, however, handled him with masterful tact. The India Office, he knew, would not hear of such a procedure. Then the scandal which Sanquo and his mother would turn to their advantage had to be considered. The whole of India would seethe with the news. The disloyalists would lie and subtly twist it to their advantage. They would set abroad the story that the British Raj had deposed the real Maharajah and substituted an impostor—a creature of their own, and that this was the beginning of the end—that other princes were to be served in like manner.

The Maharajah had seen the force of these arguments at length, and had submitted the whole management of his restoration to the others. Therefor, it had been decided, after long conversation, that stealth was to be the watch-word, and that a secret expedition into Kathnagar itself was to be undertaken.

The Chief of Police, after a reperusal of his sheaf of telegrams, agreed to this proposal, but had dilated warningly on its extreme danger. That was the last word in Harland's long review of the day's proceedings.

He glanced up. Carter sat motionless in his chair; his eyes were closed, he was fast asleep. Harland sprang up and shook him by the shoulder.

"Wake up, you old cormorant!" he said.

Carter opened his eyes and smiled blandly.

"I like to sleep when I can," he said. "I don't suppose I shall be overwhelmed with slumber during the next three or four weeks."

Later that week Harland was made aware of the importance of the mission he and Carter were engaged upon by the marked affability of certain high officials. Extreme secrecy was observed, but there was a feeling in select official circles that something important was in the wind.

And on the fourth day of that week another person made his appearance on the scene. This was Captain Taylor. Captain Taylor suddenly found himself attached to the forthcoming expedition to Kathnagar. He was a lean man, with a lean face, possessed of rather fine blue eyes, wrinkled at the corners with exposure to the sun. He was a man who did not talk—he did not believe in words—they only tired him. If it had been possible for him to live alone on an uncharted island, and to be attacked by savages from Monday morning to Saturday night, he would have been the happiest man on earth. As it was, owing to the flatness of his existence, his rather fine blue eyes had taken on an expression of settled gloom.

He was gloomy when he was introduced to Carter, and as

his gift of apprehension was not of lightning-like order, he remained gloomy for an hour afterwards.

Then he broke into sudden and disconcerting laughter, showing strong, regular, white teeth.

"No?" he cried incredulously. "Really? I don't believe it!"

Carter repeated everything he had said all over again. After that Harland reiterated the same information, and Taylor drew in a deep breath.

"Why it looks," he said, "as if there were a chance of a regular Al dust-up!"

Then, ashamed of his garrulity, and having talked himself out, he relapsed into blissful silence.

"Just the man we want," said Carter to Harland, when the lean Captain had departed. "He's spoiling for a fight, and, unless I'm a Dutchman, he'll get it!"

15

A Street in Kathnagar

The scantily-furnished, white-walled room was darkened; it was the hour of noon, and Harland had surrendered, like all the rest of that little world, to the mastery of the midday heat.

Harland, reclining on his pallet, smoked lazily. He had arrived at Kathnagar late the night before, with a certain Elwah Giuch, in whose house he was now quartered,

The details of their secret entry into Kathnagar had been arranged with the utmost minuteness. Carter's entire future depended on the success of the expedition—Sanquo had outwitted him in London, and his blood was up. He knew that the business he and Harland had undertaken possessed every possible element of danger, but the Maharajah trusted him, the India Office evidently still retained a certain amount of confidence in him; therefore there must be no mistake. Both he and Harland now gave Sanquo full credit for remarkable daring and astuteness. The contest between them was to be a contest of giants, but it was to take place in the dark. The exigencies of Indian politics demanded that this must be so. Not a word of what was about to take place in Kathnagar was to find its way into the papers.

The silent, shuttered room, in which Harland now reclined, belonged to Elwah Giuch, the elderly brother-in-law of Krishna Coomar. Giuch was a rich merchant, as loyal to the Maharajah as poor Krishna Coomar had been. At an urgent message from the Bombay Chief of Police he had visited that city, and had been made acquainted with the state of affairs. There had been a dramatic moment in the Chief of Police's house when Elwah Giuch had been presented to the Maharajah.

The elderly merchant clicked his teeth together. For a moment he believed devils were at work—he had known the Maharajah since his childhood—and the Maharajah stood before him. And yet in Kathnagar there was also a Maharajah!

Then Elwah Giuch recalled that there had been much talk in Kathnagar of the stealthy way in which the Prince had returned to his palace after visiting Europe; but underlying that talk there had not been the faintest suspicion as to the true state of affairs.

Elwah Giuch, with the deepest homage, placed himself totally at the Prince's service. At the back of his Eastern mind there may have lurked a burning desire for vengeance upon the assassin of his brother-in-law, but he permitted no such private and unimportant inclination to mar the perfect serenity of his countenance.

The first move in Carter's campaign was to employ the services of Elwah Giuch, who, under instructions, travelled back to his home in Kathnagar, accompanied by a dark-skinned friend. Harland made the same journey by the same train, passing as a tourist.

The Maharajah, in the guise of a friend of the elderly merchant, arrived safely at Giuch's house without exciting the least notice. Harland also took up his quarters in that house entirely unobserved.

It had been arranged that the Maharajah and Harland were to secrete themselves in Giuch's house until Carter was able to put his further neatly-arranged plan for securing access to Sanquo into execution.

This plan was simplicity itself, and had been devised by Carter for securing easy access to the palace of Kathnagar. Carter had cabled Quilliam that some accredited representative should be sent on a sham errand to the false Maharajah; and Quilliam, with the swift grasp of a situation that characterised him, had instantly sent letters to the palace of Kathnagar, announcing that His Majesty the King had been pleased to confer on His Highness the Maharajah of Kathnagar a Knight Companionship of the Star of India, and that Captain Taylor would have the honour to arrive very shortly to announce that honour officially to His Highness. This news having been conveyed through the proper channel to Sanquo's fraudulent Maharajah, Sanquo, off his guard, had seen that a suitable house near the palace itself was prepared for the reception of Captain Taylor and the special representative of the India Office who accompanied him.

These were the plans that had been laid, and Carter, in the guise of an official from the India Office, was expected to arrive with Taylor that night.

As the afternoon wore on, the city awoke slowly from its

enchanted dreams. The crows emerged from the shelter of the trees and came flapping and cawing into the narrow street. Light footsteps began to patter beneath Harland's window; words in strange tongues fell upon his ears. He went to the window, and flinging open the shutters, stepped on to the loggia—a little, airy, snowy-white balcony—the thin stone of which was carved into marvellous frgile patterns scarcely more tangible than lace.

Sunlight waned, and the street gradually filled. Harland continued to look down in wondering interest on a scene that surpassed anything he had imagined of the strangeness of the East. The richer members of the white-robed crowds wore silk turbans of pink, celadon-green, or sulphur-yellow; and many of the men had painted on their foreheads the sign of Siva—a white butterfly, with wings expanded from either side of a red circle. The followers of Vishnu were distinguished by a red and white trident painted between the eyebrows and rising to the hair.

"What do you think of it all?" asked a soft voice behind him, as Harland stepped back into the room.

"Wonderful," exclaimed Harland. "I thought it would have been far more Europeanised."

The Maharajah, who had entered the room silently, was dressed in soft, white, native garments, and was wearing a pair of green slippers; he took out a gold cigarette-case, offered Harland a cigarette, and took one himself. Then he seated himself on Harland's bed and smoked for a minute, staring dreamily before him. Either the return to his native country or the fact that he wore again the costume of his race appeared to give him an added seriousness and dignity. It struck Harland as strange that this quiet, dreamy-eyed man, seated on the end of his iron bedstead, was the real ruler of the jostling, gorgeous multitude that passed beneath his window that afternoon, was by birth the lord of two million subjects, with the power of life and death of an area hundreds of miles in extent.

"When I think of it," said Harland, "it takes my breath away."

The Maharajah, seated on the bed, raised his dark eyes.

"What?" he asked.

"This conspiracy against your Highness," said Harland; "The idea that a puppet impostor is posing as yourself in the palace!"

To his surprise the Maharajah merely smoked quietly for a minute, and then said: "In India such things have happened many times."

There was silence for a minute; then he rose, and, laying a brown hand on Harland's sleeve, spoke in a low, anxious voice.

"You don't think there will be any hitch? You don't think there will be any mistake—any accident?"

Harland reassured him.

"It occurred to me," went on the Prince, "that Mr. Carter might—might meet with an accident."

"I think we can trust Carter to take care of himself," said Harland, confidently.

"In that case," the Prince, "he should pass here in an hour. The bungalow selected for his residence is three miles out of the town, and is within a mile of the palace itself. Unless Sanquo's suspicions have been aroused, the carriages from the Palace will meet Carter and Captain Taylor at the station. There is a twelve-mile drive."

As the minutes sped, and Carter and Captain Taylor became due to pass through the narrow street, the Prince betrayed his anxiety by walking restlessly back and forth in the room. Elwah

Giuch put his obsequious head in at the door and asked if he could be of service to His Highness, but the Prince dismissed him with a feverish gesture, and continued his walk.

An hour passed. The Prince confronted Harland. "Something has happened," he said in a low voice.

"No, no," said Harland.

And at that moment they heard a shout from the street below.

Both the Prince and Harland hurried to the balcony—the Prince screening himself behind the shutters. For down the street they made out a Royal carriage drawn by prancing Arab horses, and driven by a coachman in the livery of the Maharajah. This man wore a gilt turban. And sat like a statue on the box, whilst two footmen, stationed at the carriage steps, ran forward, clearing the road with loud cries. The people stepped back, other traffic drew to the side of the road, and many salutations were offered as the landau moved forward.

The carriage came nearer, and passed beneath Harland's balcony. Harland saw Carter leaning back on the cushions, wearing a white suit and a sun-helmet. Beside him, in uniform, sat Captain Taylor. The carriage passed, but neither Carter nor Taylor looked up at the window.

A second Royal carriage, piled with luggage, followed, accompanied by Native servants.

The Maharajah gave a deep sigh of relief and stepped back into the room.

16

The House of the Silver Lily

Carter reclined at his ease in the Maharajah's landau, as the vehicle dashed forward, scattering the throng in the main street of Kathnagar. Like a good general he had planned every detail of his campaign. He had decided that the action he would take must be swift and decisive; he must strike his blow before Sanquo had time to suspect.

There was to be no publicity. On that condition, a much-agitated Quilliam had cabled him *carte blanche*. He was empowered to dispossess the usurping Amoola Khan and capture Sanquo in any manner that suited him. The Secretary for India knew the danger of the adventure upon which Carter and Harland had embarked, and it was perfectly understood that in the advent of any disaster happening to either, the British Government would disclaim all knowledge of their existence.

The work of restoring the Maharaja of Kathnagar had taken on the character of a secret mission, and every Government in Europe notoriously abandons its secret agents in times of peril and discovery. Carter was fully aware of the risks he ran. He was fully aware of the mental power and subtlety of the man against whom he had pitted himself, and took extraordinary precautions in consequence. Harland, for his part, welcomed the possibility of adventure with boyish eagerness.

Captain Taylor, that blameless, monosyllabic, lean soldier, peered stolidly from beneath his topee, eyed the country, and inwardly appraised its sporting possibilities. As the carriage drew out of the town and plunged along the blood-red road, he occasionally pointed out to Carter landmarks and houses of wealthy Natives.

"What sort of place is this bungalow of the Silver Lily?" asked Carter.

Taylor looked at him with an appearance of thoughtfulness. Taylor's faculty of looking deceptively intelligent was one of his chief social assets. But he was unilluminating on the subject of the bungalow to which they were driving. It was just a bungalow like any other; rather large perhaps. Of course one storey high, a verandah round it; generally allotted to distinguished European visitors. If Carter wanted to see a house that really *was* a house, he ought to hop up to the British Resident's place at Maliwar.

"What was the British Resident there like?"

For some minutes Carter dug monosyllables out of Taylor, and arrived at the information that Taylor's late superior was a fifth-rate billiard player, a second-rate shot, and a first-rate cocktail drinker; he had a wife with a skin like a lemon and a voice like a macaw; and that whenever he found a victim, he would play poker from dinner till dawn.

The carriage plunged along, and the agile brown footmen,

who in the crowded thoroughfare had raced along at its side gesticulating and clearing the road, were now squatting comfortably on its steps.

"There you are!" said Taylor, garrulously, after a quarter of an hour.

He raised a sun-tanned hand and pointed to a low-lying patch of white glinting through a sparse clump of trees. As they drew nearer, Carter made out a large, white brick house with a broad verandah. The house was surrounded by a little garden laid out in European fashion. The efforts of the gardeners, however, had been somewhat frustrated by the fertility of the Indian soil.

Half-a-dozen Native servants came pouring through the gate as the carriage stopped. They were swift, dexterous fellows; and the butler, a big-faced adipose, grave man, in voluminous white robes, made many salaams, and conducted Carter and Taylor along the garden path to a heavy green door which stood open, giving ingress to the cool shade of the house. This man, Kalim, was an old servant of the Maharajah's and spoke very creditable English.

Carter and Taylor—blinking in the sudden transition from sunlight to shadow—made out in the living room a dim figure, who spoke soft, mellifluous words, and offered a grave, exaggerated Eastern salutation on behalf of His Highness, who to-morrow would have the great honour to receive them at the palace. This gentleman was the Maharajah's Minister of State, a superb, aquiline-nosed Native of magnificent and immense lineage. He received them, delivered his message, and departed like a spirit.

Later in the evening, when the Maharajah himself and Harland arrived at the house in the guise of servants, Kalim admitted them, and showed them the rooms set apart for their occupation.

Kalim was entirely unsuspicious. He received them with the dignity due to his position, and having acquainted Carter of their arrival, permitted them to present themselves to their masters. Carter and Taylor, who were on the verandah, rose instantly and entered the drawing-room. The lamp on the buhl desk was lit, and the window shutters closed.

In another minute the four men were alone together.

"Well?" questioned the Prince, anxiously.

He stood in the middle of the room, rubbing his hands nervously together, his eyes fixed upon Carter.

"Thank God you arrived safely," said Carter, in a low voice. "We were received here by your Highness's Minister of State, and are to receive a message in the morning saying what time we are to present ourselves at the palace. I think," he went on, "it would not be wise to discuss things here."

"The walls are two feet thick," said the Maharajah, with a smile.

"Even walls two feet thick may have ears," answered Carter. "Who is this fellow Kalim?"

"A very honest servant," answered the Maharajah. "If I were to reveal myself to him—"

"Your Highness has placed this matter in my hands," went on Carter, still speaking under his breath.

"Yes, yes," protested the Prince; "but—"

"I think we all realise that we are dealing with a man whose gifts it is dangerous to underestimates," said Carter. "Sanquo at the present moment holds all the cards. I think your Highness understands that."

The Prince took his gold cigarette-case from his pocket, drew out a cigarette, and was about to light it, but, remembering his role of servant, replaced the case in his pocket.

"Perfectly," he said at last. "I place myself entirely in your hands."

That night, when the Prince and Taylor had retired, Carter and Harland sat together in the drawing-room, smoking and talking. The room was lighted only by the shaded lamp on the heavy, expensive buhl desk.

In the drawer of the buhl desk Taylor had placed, under lock and key, the documents setting forth His Majesty's gracious desire to create the Maharajah of Kathnagar a Knight Commander of the Star of India.

"Harland," said Carter, "did you notice the Prince's inclination to reveal himself to that fellow Kalim?"

Harland nodded.

"It is quite what I expected," went on Cater. "He is growing restless. It is only natural he should. We must keep a tight hold on him, or we shall have him firing the mine before we are ready. Then there'll be the devil to pay! As far as I can make out there is not a soul in the whole State who has a suspicion as to the identity of the fellow Sanquo has put up."

Half an hour later, when Harland also had gone to bed, and the whole house was in darkness, Carter, feeling a little uneasy at the responsibility of the situation, took a lamp from the drawing-room and made a cautious tour of the rooms. Kalim was the only servant who slept in the house. Carter cautiously tried the doors and the windows; they were all carefully secured. He returned to the drawing-room, extinguished the lamp, then, locking the door, went to his own room.

Harland was also in his room, a little apartment next to Carter, his supposed master. The absence of a lock on his door did not disturb Harland, although he took the precaution of placing an upturned chair against it.

Carter, however, was more suspicious. His bedroom door was also without a lock. He struck a match and examined the lintel. The lock had been removed, and the screw-holes filled with putty, coloured to match the paint. It was singular that the putty had not yet hardened. Carter made that discovery by probing it with the point of his pocket-knife. Then he sat down on his bed-side and began to think. No sound reached his ears save the strange, busy murmur of far-away insects and the occasional cry of a distant night bird. He sat in complete darkness and listened.

In the meantime Harland, having gone to bed, became dissatisfied with the angle of the chair he had placed against the door. He foresaw that a slight draught against the door might send it down, and startle him from his sleep. Therefore he rose and, removing the chair, stood at his door pondering a better method of fastening it.

Suddenly he flung up his head and listened.

Somebody was walking very softly in the interior of the house. He heard distinct, gentle footfalls, which appeared to move forward a few paces cautiously, and then to stop. Once a period of five minutes elapsed, during which a heavy silence reigned in the house. Then came a continuance of the footfalls— and again silence. Harland retreated into his room, and drew on his clothes swiftly and silently.

Suddenly a thin beam of light shone from the house on to the trees in the garden and disappeared. Harland put a cautious hand to his hip pocket, and, stepping out on to the broad verandah, began to make a detour of the house. He passed Carter's window, stepping softly.

Harland at length came to the closed shutters of the drawing-room, and stopped. He knew that Carter had locked the drawing-room door and had gone to bed; yet there was a light there now. He waited a minute in the stillness, then bent forward and looked in.

Instantly the light within disappeared.

"Don't make a sound," said a low voice in his ear.

"You startled me out of my skin," whispered Harland, turning to face Carter, who was fully dressed, and stood behind him, his face grave in the darkness.

"What is it?" asked Carter.

"A light that vanished," said Harland. "I heard footsteps in the house; then I saw a light flash across the trees and thought I'd investigate. You locked the drawing-room door?"

"Yes," answered Carter. "The key's in my pocket. I was sitting on my bed, thinking, when you passed my window. Have you noticed that the bedroom locks have been removed?"

"Yes," whispered Harland, "do you think the Prince is safe?"

"I've set Taylor to keep guard over his door," answered Carter. "Sanquo's in this, of course; but it may be that he is merely cautious, and wants to find out if we are really what we say we are. Kalim is the only person sleeping in the house except ourselves. Are you sure there was a light?"

Harland nodded in the darkness.

"We must keen an eye on Kalim" said Carter, and slipping off his shoes moved into the house, pausing at last before Kalim's bedroom door. He listened there for a moment; then, drawing a match from his pocket, inserted it in the interstice between the door and the lintel. Having accomplished this, he took a second match and placed it a hand's span above the first. He inserted three matches in this fashion, one above the other, a hand's span apart. It Kalim's door opened the matches would fall, and it would be impossible for him to replace them, as he would not know at what distance apart they had been originally inserted.

Carter returned to Harland as cautiously as he had gone.

"That accounts of Kalim," he said. "Now we will watch the outside of the house."

For many minutes after that he and Harland stood motionless, invisible in the shadow of the verandah, each in such a position that he could watch one end and one side of the house. Thus it was impossible for anyone to leave the building without their cognisance.

They had watched for half an hour, when the gloom of the night on the garden side was again swept by a moving blade of light. No sound had reached their ears. It was Harland who saw the light, which issued from the drawing-room as before. This time he took infinite pains to avoid making a sound, and again he peered through the blind.

The drawing-room lamp, which Carter had extinguished, was lighted, and standing at the buhl table, with a bunch of keys in her hand, was a bent, brown-faced woman, wearing a snow-white sari. She was between fifty and sixty years of age; her bent body teemed with vitality and energy. She shot the keys through her fingers with the swiftness of legerdemain. A moment later she drew up a chair and seated herself at the desk, holding a particular key in her fingers. One after the other she opened the drawers of the buhl desk, inserting in each a deft, questing hand. At length she drew forth the drawer containing Taylor's credentials and Quilliam's document on India Office paper, announcing the honour which His Majesty proposed to confer on the Maharajah. She laid the papers one after the other, on the desk-top, and, removing them cautiously from the envelope, leaned forward and read them closely in the light of the lamp. Her strong, bronze profile was sharply outlined.

As she read the papers, one after the other, Harland saw her nod her head, apparently in satisfaction.

Once she looked up sharply, as a startled tiger may look up from its prey. Her eyes sought the door, then the window. For a fraction of time she and Harland were eye to eye. The full burning brightness of her gaze held his for a moment. He knew that he was invisible to her but the hard glitter of those eyes was not a pleasant thing to see, and he was not sorry that Carter, who had also seen the light gleaming across the bushes in the garden, was now standing beside him, participating in his view of the mysterious visitant.

The woman, having scrutinised the documents, began to replace them in the drawer.

"Harland," whispered Carter, I'll leave it to you to catch her. A good wrench at the window and you'll be inside! I'll watch the outside of the house, in case she is not alone."

Harland nodded, and Carter moved silently away. The woman in white sari had closed and was locking the drawer when Harland suddenly shattered the silence by bursting open the window.

Without a start of surprise, without looking at him, the woman leaned forward and blew out the lamp. But Harland was in the room. Through the heavy darkness he could see her vaguely, a faint, hazy, white form, moving swiftly towards the door. But he had expected this manœuvre, and was there before her.

She turned and moved swiftly towards a dark corner of the room. Then, as he sprang after her, a strange thing happened— the dim white outline of her sari grew still, quivered, and descending into the floor, disappeared.

As Harland struck a match he heard further stealthy movements, In the flare of light he glanced about him. The door was open behind him, and at his feet—a pool of white muslin— lay the woman's discarded sari.

She had tricked him by slipping it off and doubling towards the door.

He lit the lamp, and running along the passage searched the interior of the house. There was no sign of an intruder, only Taylor, taciturn, at the Maharajah's door; no sound broke the stillness. The three matches, a hand's span apart, remained in Kalim's door exactly as Carter had placed them.

For a few minutes Harland stood in the rush-covered hall listening and glancing about him.

It was then that he heard a sound as of two pieces of iron clanking together. Later, when he had confessed his failure to capture the woman to Carter, they decided to watch all night. Carter himself had seen no one—no one had attempted to leave the house.

Carter and Harland watched the outside of the house throughout the small hours of the night, and until the babel of voices from the servants' quarters told them that a new day had commenced. Theirs was a fruitless vigil, however, and equally fruitless was the close search of the interior of the house, made in the company of Kalim in the early hours of the morning. The old woman, who possessed a duplicate key of the drawing-room and duplicate keys of the buhl desk, had made no attempt to escape from the house, and was yet not discovered within it.

Kalim was at his wits end. He stared in bewilderment at the white sari found in the drawing-room, but when Harland spoke of the clanking of iron upon iron he had heard in the night a curious thoughtful look came into the Native's eyes.

Both Carter and Harland noticed that look.

17

The Audience

Carter was dozing in a rush chair on the verandah, after his vigil of the night. Presently the clatter of hoofs assailed his ears, and a horseman, bearing an invitation to the palace, reined in at the gate.

Kalim presented himself on the verandah and made obeisance to Carter, who took from his hand a letter sealed with the Maharajah's own seal—an elephant and two peacocks. A slight smile crossed Carter's features as he looked at the broad disc of scarlet wax and thought of the two rascals, the greater and the less—Sanquo and Amoola Khan—who had managed to secure that emblem of sovereignty and power.

Taylor in full uniform—as pretty a picture of highly-burnished soldier as one might wish to see—sat beside Carter during the drive to the Royal Palace of Kathnagar. He held on his knees the two large envelopes which contained Quilliam's messages to the Maharajah and his own and Carter's credentials.

Harland and the Maharajah watched the carriage drive away.

In the Maharajah's fingers lay the letter summoning Carter to the palace, the letter stamped with his own seal, feloniously used. As the sound of the carriage wheels died away he smiled a little as he scrutinised the fractured red disc. It was a peculiar smile, a smile which disfigured his refined features and brought a fierce light into his gentle, dark brown eyes. He folded the letter with great care and placed it in his pocket. ...

Ecstasy, rapture, artistic appreciation were all entirely outside Carter's nature, but it was beyond his power to suppress a gasp of surprise when the Royal Palace of Kathnagar suddenly appeared before him at a turn in the road. The cold fact that this palace is larger than any European palace, that a million pounds worth of chiselled marble, jade, and lapis lazuli have been lavished on its surface, conveys nothing more than an idea of Oriental prodigality. But the Palace itself, a vision of rose-pink, glowing delicately against a sky of azure, is a thing of beauty such as is to be found in no other country in the world. The splendour of its five hundred twinkling windows, of its eight gold-veined miniarets, the slender grace of its lofty, Moorish-windowed tower, impress themselves on the imagination as exotic, Eastern, dream-like, and wonder-inspiring.

When the carriage, after traversing a drive that might have admitted to an English country house, drew up at length on the stone pavement at the foot of a flight of white marble steps, Carter and Taylor alighted to receive the salutations of the aristocratic Minister of State, whom they had seen the day previously. A squad of the Maharajah's soldiers stood at attention, their bayonets gleaming in the dazzling sunlight.

As the Minister led Carter and Taylor up the marble steps towards the great burnished brass doors of the palace, doors which glowed sullenly in the reflected light from the marble steps, three or four tame cheetahs, wearing silver muzzles, moved languidly aside, and again squatted on the warm steps, watching them with bright amber eyes.

Carter was wondering consumedly how Sanquo would play his part, for as yet there was no sign of him. The burnished doors opened noiselessly; then, still following the dignified Minister, of State, Carter and Taylor found themselves suddenly in the strange greenish gloom of a vast mosaic-floored chamber. Having crossed the great echoing chamber, they came at last to a little flight of black marble steps. Two tall Pathans, with grounded rifles, eyed them as they passed. A door opened, and they found themselves in the Presence Chamber. In a Chair of State, placed before a gold curtain, was seated Amoola Khan, wearing stark-white garments and a scarlet turban. On either side of him stood a grey-haired Native holding a slender white staff.

Carter glanced sharply about him, for a sign of Sanquo, but that astute gentleman was not present.

Amoola Khan rose and came forward with a simplicity and graciousness that would have been commendable in the real ruler of Kathnagar.

"Captain Taylor," he said cordially, and extended his hand, "I am most pleased to see you again."

"Blazing insolence!" babbled Taylor inwardly.

Amoola Khan extended a similar courtesy towards Carter, who gripped his hand heartily. He exhibited a remarkable resemblance to the real Maharajah, and showed every evidence of having been educated at a good school in England. Carter wondered how it came that he was willing to risk his life at Sanquo's bidding.

But where was Dr. Sanquo? Would he deem it advisable to show himself at this interview?

The formalities between Amoola Khan and Captain Taylor occupied a quarter of an hour, and it was not until they were concluded that Amoola Khan beckoned to his side the lean, aquiline Minister of State, and spoke to him in Hindoostani.

The Minister of State, on his part, opened the black door by which they had entered and transferred the message to one of the Pathans on guard there.

"I should like," said Amoola Khan suavely, to Captain Taylor, "to introduce you to my new medical adviser."

Taylor bowed.

Carter broke the silence: "Your Highness must feel deeply the loss of your old tutor, Krishna Coomar."

He looked steadily into the other's eyes, but Amoola Khan merely shook his head and passed his slender ringed hands one over the other.

The door opened, and Dr. Sanquo entered. He stood within the threshold waiting to be summoned forwards.

"Gad," thought Taylor, "the fellow plays his part devilish well!"

Amoola Khan a few minutes later appeared to become conscious of the Doctor's presence, and, graciously beckoning him forward introduced him first to Taylor, then to Cater. Carter was interested to notice that the Doctor still retained his alias of Sanquo.

It was the first time he and this arch-rascal had stood together face to face. The Doctor's bold, narrow-eyed face looked darker in contrast with his white linen suit. His manner was confident. Whatever had been the circumstances of their meeting—if Sanquo had been the greatest pattern of benevolence in the world—Carter and he would have been enemies instinctively. Sanquo was conscious of this as Carter momentarily held his fingers in a firm handshake. He knew, in some subtle, intuitive fashion that the man before him was portentious and dangerous.

Cater for his part seemed in that moment better able to understand the capacity of the man against whom he had pitted himself. He gave Sanquo credit for outwitting him in London, but he plumed himself not a little on the knowledge that until that moment Sanquo had not been conscious of his existence.

Their hands fell apart—the incident was at an end. But Sanquo felt a natural desire to see more of this man he disliked, this handsome, tall emissary from the India Office. With the swift, conscious appraisement of a man judging an inferior in intellect, he dismissed Taylor as negligible. But Carter was a man to fathom, a man to question—and perhaps a man to watch.

Amoola Khan, with a magnificence which caused Taylor to ejaculate inwardly, "Damn his insolence!" announced that he desired their company at dinner one night that week, and that there would be a *fête* in the gardens afterwards. Also, following the custom usually extended to distinguished visitors, he informed them that his Minister of State was awaiting their pleasure to inspect the palace—that is, the main state-rooms of the palace, the zenana of course being inviolable.

It fell out that Dr. Sanquo, and not the Minister of State, showed them through the various rooms. Taylor, who had seen it all before, suppressed his yawns and clattered along, the picture of ill-concealed boredom. Carter, however, was vastly wide awake; this was exactly what he had hoped for. He could scarcely suppress a smile at the manner in which his antagonist was playing into his hands. To have your enemy invite you into his beleagured city and show you all the weak points of his defence is a piece of good fortune that seldom falls to a combatant.

Carter's naïve curiosity, his trick of opening windows and looking out, his fondness for opening and shutting doors, puzzled Sanquo, but appeared to arouse no suspicion in him.

The Maharajah's sleeping apartments were on the first floor, overlooking a large fountain copied from Versailles. In the distance, beyond this fountain, stood a long-storeyed building, the Maharajah's private tiger-house. This building was an improved copy of the lion-house at the London Zoo, and was inhabited by fifteen tigers, some of whom had been recently captured, a dozen wolves, leopards and cheetahs.

The Maharajah's state bedchamber opened into a passage which ran the entire length of the palace, and came to an end at a curtain beyond which began a passage leading to the zenana, inviolable to all save the Maharajah himself.

Carter took in the details of this room with particular interest, and as he politely saved Sanquo the trouble of closing the door when they stepped into the passage again, he noticed its peculiar thickness. The lock, however, was a trivial gilt affair, brought from Paris. Carter left the palace, however, with the thought in his mind that a Maharajah does not depend upon locks for his nightly protection.

❖

The *fête* promised by Amoola Khan took place some evenings later, and when the House of the Silver Lily awoke from its midday siesta, the dusty red road from Kathnagar to the Maharajah's palace began to grow populous with a streaming multitude, the first comers of the advance guard intent on securing good places from which to obtain a view of the Royal fireworks.

Harland was watching the scene with keen interest when he noticed a short, bent figure on the far side of the road attempting to breast the tide which swept only in the direction of the Maharajah's palace. The figure became noticeable by the very fact that it was the only one moving in that direction.

Something familiar in the contour of the lowered, muslin-swathed head caught Harland's eye. He plunged into the throng, and worked his way to the far side of the road. The figure was some distance away now, making its slow progress forward; many animated townsfolk separated it from Harland, but he pressed in pursuit, and a minute later laid his hand on the shoulder of a bent old woman, who turned a sharp, aquiline face towards him and eyed him with a swift, suspicious glance.

Harland's grip remained quite firm on her shoulder.

"You got away neatly three nights ago," he said. "How did you get out of the house? And what did you want with those papers?"

The look of keen intelligence in the woman's eyes began to fade away. She blinked at him, stupidly, and answered in plaintive Hindoostani. Harland ordered her to answer in English. She shook her head vacantly, and broke out again in Hindoostani.

"You appear to be able to *read* English clearly if you can't speak it," said Harland, sharply.

The woman made deprecating gestures—she was plainly wondering what the sahib could want with her—a poor, harmless woman making her way with such pathetic difficulty against this great horde of sight-seers.

"What were you doing in that house with keys you had no right to?"

But the woman stared at him with imploring, bewildered eyes. She talked and made loose, pointless gestures with her hands—she appeared to be on the point of tears—a scene was imminent and Harland was at a loss. A scene between himself and a Native woman in that crowd was a danger and an impossibility. He wondered if the woman guessed as much, and was trying to bring it about. He looked at her again; her cringing attitude and vacant stare baffled him. His hand had already slipped from her shoulder; he hesitated a moment, then turned and made his way back to Carter, who was still at the gate.

"That was the woman who was in the drawing-room three nights ago."

"The devil it was!" said Carter. "It might be worth while strolling in her wake for a time."

Being tall men, they were able to keep her in view over the heads of the crowd. She glanced back once or twice as they advanced, but it was doubtful if she saw them. After about ten minutes of progress she turned from the animated road into a lane branching at a right angle. Waiting in this lane was a strange, egg-shaped, zebu-drawn vehicle. Stream of sightseers flowed on, obliterating Carter and Harland where they stood looking over the heads of the crowd. The little old woman, without assistance, climbed into the strange-shaped vehicle. She put out her head and called the driver, who came into view for the first time. He was a tall, muscular fellow, with a sparse black beard. Harland knew him in an instant.

"That's Hajiz!" he exclaimed to Carter. "The man who helped Sanquo to lash me to the bed in the Golden Pavilion."

18

Sanquo Overshadowed

Harland was right in his surmise, and under Hajiz's persuasion, the old woman's zebus stirred in their eternal sleep, and moved dreamily along the quiet lane. Presently Hajiz heard at his back the rattle of brass rings as the curtains of the vehicle were drawn aside; he knew that his mistress had thrust out her vulture nose and was looking at the hurrying crowd, now growing nebulous as the cart drew further from it. Her small eyes glowered into the distance, her lips moved rapidly. She rubbed her shoulder, and cursed Harland's present and future in pious native formula with astounding venom and energy. Then suddenly she withdrew her head, closed the curtains, and vanished into the interior of the cart.

The zebus ambled forward in contemptuous indifference to Hajiz and the whole world.

The cart made a detour, and at last drew up before a house in the suburbs of Kathnagar. The old woman, with a rapid look to right and left, descended cautiously from her vehicle and passed through the house into a small room overlooking a garden at the back.

Half-an-hour later Sanquo strode into that room, carrying his topee in his hand. A curious something lit in the old woman's eyes as she looked upon his tall, agile figure. In Sanquo's expression, too, a subtle change took place. If it were possible for his features to contain a look of tenderness, that look was there now.

"Well, my mother?" he questioned.

Gunara Tukaji put up her arms and embraced him; then with a characteristic, imperious, swift gesture of the hand, indicated that he should seat himself. He drew a creaking wicker chair towards the divan and sank back in it. He was watching her face with absorbed, concentrated gaze.

"Well?" repeated Sanquo again. This time there was a faint note of impatience underlying his question.

"All is well, my son." Sanquo had spoken in English, but she answered in Hindoostani. "There nights ago I went in through the compound and opened the door with my key. The papers were in the buhl cabinet, as we had suspected. I examined them all. There was no doubt of Quilliam's signature. Taylor's credentials and those also of the other man are in perfect order."

In the pause that followed her last words her lips tightened, a look of fierce resentment leapt into her eyes.

"This is not work for me," she said. "I am too old for rash things. The white servant of this man Carter burst in through the window upon me. I escaped only because I knew the house well. To-day that same servant knew me again, and gripped me by the shoulder on the road. You bring these things upon me, my son, by your want of strength. In your haste to move quickly, you neglect to prepare the ground." She suddenly turned her eyes full on him and held him with her gaze. "I fear, sometimes, my Henry, that you are like that fool, your father. I had hoped you would follow me; I had hoped the gods would allow me to work out my destiny through you. There is the warmth of the East in my veins, the ambition of Greatness in my bones. I have planned a mighty future for you. If Vishnu had brought me to earth a man, I would have held this India in my strong arms as a mother holds a child. I would have built up an Empire greater than the Empire of the Moguls. I would have plucked out this little white thorn that stings our flesh."

She was a woman born with mighty ambitions. As a girl of high caste in Benares, she sought to realise her dreams by laying her finger on the heart of Addison, the wealthy Scotch merchant. Her beauty at that time was said to have been amazing. She moulded men as a potter moulds clay. Never for a moment could Addison have denied her a thing she called upon him to do. Like the old scheming Empress of China—who also rose from obscurity—she never rested, never ceased to intrigue, never ceased to spread sedition, and the hopes of a glorious Eastern future for India—for a new Indian Empire.

She was disappointed in her son; he was merely a brilliant scoundrel, but he was the best tool she had been able to find. No one ever knew the real heart of this woman—whether a true love of India actuated her ambition, or whether she coveted power for its own sake.

She fell into silence at last. Sanquo spoke again.

"I suspected this mission, my mother," he said, "because of its suddenness. It seemed strange that the Government should suddenly thrust an honour on the Maharajah in this fashion."

The old woman raised a peremptory hand.

"Your own feebleness is to blame!" she retorted. "If you had worked boldly and swiftly, as one who is chosen of Destiny, there would have been no ground for suspicion."

Sanquo venture to interrupt her.

"I told you before, my mother, There was no time to do away with him. You don't understand the conditions in England. If I had delayed another hour in London, I should have been seized by the police, and the whole scheme would have come to nothing."

"As it is," said the old woman, fiercely, "you are in fear every day that he may escape and make himself known."

"There is no fear of that," said Sanquo. "I have paid men to watch the ship; if he attempts to get to India—"

The old woman peered at him with hard, narrow eyes and uttered an exclamation of contempt under her breath. She clasped her beautiful brown hands tightly together.

"If Vishnu had but made me a man!" she said.

During a long silence she smoked, and peered out towards the cool green of the garden.

"Amoola Khan is wax in our hands," she said at length, in her drowsy voice. "He is the little puppet who dances to our string—he is the silken glove that hides our strong hand."

She suddenly turned her eyes on Sanquo; her words became sharp and staccato: "We never were so near success as now. Now is the time to move with soft footsteps and silent tread. The machines are safe?"

"They are in the vault beneath the palace," answered Sanquo. He rose and walked to the window. "The Resident's a fool," he said, "and we can afford to forget him. But I wish this mission were over—this visit from Taylor and the man from the India Office."

"I suspect nothing there," said his mother, smoking steadily.

"I have seen the man Carter before," said Sanquo, turning towards her. "I cannot recollect where."

"You doubt him?"

"No."

The old woman's eyes were upon him; she caught the faint note of hesitancy in his voice and strove to dispel the suspicion.

"I have told you his papers were in order. But this servant of his," she went on, "I do not like." Sanquo glanced at her questioningly. "It was he who seized me by the shoulder to-day;" an evil light came into her eyes. "He is arrogance itself, that one," she said. "Last night when I examined his luggage, while he and his master watched for me outside the bungalow, I found his dressing-case more expensive than his master's. What do you make of that, my Henry?"

"You mistook the bag of the servant for that of the master," said Sanquo with a smile.

"The servant's bag was in the servant's room," went on the mother, quietly; "moreover, the name he is known by at the bungalow is not the name I found upon the letters addressed to him inside his case."

"What?" exclaimed Sanquo, quickly, swift suspicion leaping into his eyes. Then he turned to the window and stared out, remaining silent for a minute.

"What was the name upon the letters?" he asked, in a steady, casual voice.

"Harland—Philip Harland," answered the old woman, and she continued to smoke steadily.

Sanquo had not moved, but his averted face had changed swiftly. A strong likeness to his mother became apparent.

"Well, my son, what is it that makes you afraid?" she jeered.

Sanquo turned on her swiftly and fiercely.

The name of Philip Harland conveyed nothing to her, but to him it conveyed everything. For the next few minutes his personality dominated hers. He poured out to her in full that which she already knew in part—the history of Harland's pursuit of him in London. He admitted to her that he had underestimated Harland, had counted him a fool. When at length he ceased his narrative and grew silent again, his mother rose softly from her divan, and coming to him where he stood at the window, laid a hand on his shoulder. The singular light in her vivid eyes, the eloquence of her low, vibrant voice, magnetised him.

"Listen, my son," she whispered ...

An hour later Sanquo left the house of Gunara Tukaji and leapt into his saddle.

Away from his mother he grew more resolute, more self-reliant, more watchful. In a sense her superior mentality oppressed him, and appeared to blunt his faculties. This evening, however, his watchfulness failed him in slight degree. As he turned the corner of the road some hundred yards from his mother's house he glanced among the trees which shadowed the path to right and to the left.

He saw no one there, and another pawn went to Carter in this strange game which Fate was playing with the lives of men.

19

A Watchful Mother

The Residency of Kathnagar was a fine, comfortable building, strategically situated, not too far away from the palace to be out of touch with the doings therein, and not too near to appear inquisitively close. The main feature of the Residency was the garden beloved of Lady Strickley, who, hard woman as she was, had yet a tender place in her heart for the glory of an Eastern Garden.

The day preceding that on which Sanquo learned the astounding news that Harland was at the House of the Silver Lily, disguised as a servant, Lady Strickley spent the cool of the evening surveying the ordered grandeur of the Residency garden. Finally, having dismissed from her presence Raheem, the gnarled old keeper of the garden, she ascended to the verandah.

Sir Boris was stretched upon a reclining chair, wearing a thin silk suit. A light silk rug lay at his feet; a medicine bottle, a tall glass, and a few straws occupied a little table at his side.

"Boris," she said—they were alone in the privacy of the big verandah—"Boris, I've been thinking."

Sir Boris rolled his head, and looked at her with lacklustre eyes. He had nothing to say, and he eyed her in silence.

"I've been thinking," said Lady Strickley, "about the singular behaviour of the India Office."

"Singular?" questioned Strickley.

"It was singular of them," answered his wife, "to suddenly order you back here again. It was singular of them to suddenly break your leave. A few months ago they were saying in Calcutta that you were past work."

Strickley drew himself up on his chair.

"It is quite natural that they should turn to me," he said, "when this mix-up about the Maharajah arose. No one knows Kathnagar as I know it; no one knows these people as I know them."

"Don't speak quite so loud, Boris."

Lady Strickley laid a hand on her husband's wrist and glanced about her. Not only walls, but luxurious, think-foliaged gardens have ears in India.

"Well," went on Sir Boris, in a lower tone, "they wanted me to be here to see matters were arranged without publicity. If I hadn't had the forethought to warn them, the whole blame would have come on my shoulders. Many a poor fellow who has given his whole life to the Government of India has been snapped off like a twig, just because he hasn't had the subtlety to see through the trickery and chicanery that lurks in all these Native States. I happened to be quick enough to see what was going on, so I saved my skin, and I expect the Calcutta authorities are beginning to feel a bit foolish—"

"Yes, yes!" broke in Lady Strickley impatiently. "You did splendidly, Boris! But what I want to talk about is the real reason for our returning here."

"Real reason?" questioned Strickley.

"We were not ordered back here on your account, Boris," said Lady Strickley, suddenly, "nor on mine."

Strickley looked at her and smiled. The idea that she should couple herself with him in this connection struck him as an amusing piece of feminine presumption.

"In that case," he said, "why were we ordered back here?"

"We were ordered back here because Anastasia happens to be an exceptionally beautiful girl; because the India Office, represented by that horrid Dacent Smith, is capable of anything! Don't you see how things are? Surely, Boris, you are not as blind as you appear to be? Everything is as clear to me as daylight. The very week you obtained your leave and left for home the Maharajah found it necessary, for the sake of his health, and for the sake of studying international policy, that he, too should travel to England. As long as we remained in London the Maharajah remained in London, and the minute we returned to Kathnagar the Maharajah returned! Now," went on Lady Strickley, "I have made up my mind! I intend to speak to Anastasia to-night. It's scandalous that the Maharajah should dare to raise his eyes to her!"

"Eh?" barked Sir Boris. He sat up quickly, as though his wife had stuck a pin in him. "What's that you say?"

"The Maharajah is in love with Anastasia!"

"In love?"

"If you weren't as blind as a bat you'd have seen it long ago!"

"Oh!" gasped Strickley with immense relief, "is that all?" He paused a moment, then spoke with a casual air. "If you knew as much about India as I do," he said, "you'd know that a Native prince is in love with every good-looking European woman he sees! Generally the plump ones," he added with a smile. "Our women," he went on sententiously, "appeal to the Native fancy; there's a sort of romance connected with a beautiful English woman in their eyes."

Lady Strickley was waiting impatiently. Sir Boris was not a good talker, but he was a determined one, and when once the slow wheels of his mind had started moving, he was not to be stopped easily. When he had talked himself to a standstill, Lady Strickley launched her thunderbolt.

"Boris," she said, "it's my duty as Anastasia's mother to send her back home at once!"

"Nonsense!" said Sir Boris masterfully.

"She's in love with the Maharajah—I'm certain of it! What's more she's over head and ears in love with him! I've been watching her for the past few days. You don't know—you don't understand these things as I do"—her voice softened a little. "She said to me last night that she had never really felt the beauty of the garden until now. And I watched her later when the moon rose. She was standing at her window looking out; she shivered at little, and when I called her and she turned to me, I saw that tears were in her eyes. Something must be done, Boris."

Sir Boris raised himself in his chair and strode towards the door of the house He waved his hand at his wife as he went.

"Nonsense," he said, "nonsense; there's nothing in it! But if it'll satisfy you at all I'll talk to Anastasia myself about it."

"You'll talk to her! You'll do nothing of the kind!" said Lady Strickley, following him. "I tell you she's in love. Anastasia is capable of love—I know that. You're not to interfere in this matter. Boris. I forbid you!"

Later when husband and wife disappeared into the house a brown, gnarled man moved from the shadow of a tree near the verandah and stepped noiselessly into the dark jungle of the garden. He was a little, old, bent man, an ancient gardener, with startlingly bright eyes, a high forehead, and a small peaked chin. As he went he chattered softly to himself in liquid tones. The words that issued almost noiselessly from his lips were garbled English sounds, grotesquely reminiscent of the barking voice of Sir Boris and of the firm, clear tones of Lady Strickley.

That night Anastasia Strickley, arrayed in a white dinner dress, retired to her room, closed the shutters, and dismissed her woman.

"To-night I shall not need you, Pretarbi," she said in a low voice.

A few minutes later the door handle clicked, and Anastasia turned, to find her mother on the threshold. Lady Strickley closed the door.

"Where is Pretarbi?" she asked.

"I sent her away; I don't need her to-night, mother."

Lady Strickley crossed the room.

"Sit down, Anastasia," she said. "I want to talk to you."

Anastasia glanced swiftly into her mother's face. Her heart-beats quickened apprehensively; she knew not why.

" I find you looking a little pale," went on Lady Strickley, "the heat of Kathnagar is not good for you. I have therefore arranged with your father that you and I should return home."

"To England?"

It was Anastasia who spoke. A singular stillness had fallen

upon her like a mantel, and her heart, which had begun to beat apprehensively, quickened to a wild throbbing.

"If we go the day after to-morrow," said Lady Strickley, "we can catch the next boat."

20

A Love Interlude

Anastasia glanced at the little clock on her dressing-table, and as her eyes rose again she met her own glance in the depths of the mirror. The pallor of her face had fled, a deep rose-red tide of colour glorified her cheeks, her eyes shone; she was conscious again of the beating of her heart. This time it beat in wild, throbbing tumult. Joy and pain mingled indistinguishably. She crossed the room, put out the light, and for a minute paused—a faint white figure in the darkness.

She moved softly to the shuttered window, drew aside the shutters, and listened for a moment. Then, taking an enveloping dark cloak from her wardrobe, passed out on to the verandah. Keeping close to the wall of the house and out of view of the watchman, squatting in the garden at the front of the house, she moved softly forward. A minute later she was upon the smooth path below the verandah, had flitted noiselessly forward, and was lost to view. Save for the pallid oval of her face she was invisible as she moved, here and there, among the heavy shadows of the trees.

Presently she emerged before a pale sheet of light. The whisper of moving water came to her. Below her lay a pond, an artificial pond, with a marble basin, and low marble wall.

"Rao," she whispered, "Rao," and the next moment was folded in his arms. Her surrender to his embrace was absolute, complete and, unresisting.

Then suddenly she held herself from him. The Maharajah's face beneath his turban was darkly visible.

"I had great difficulty to get to you to-night," he whispered. "My good friends Carter and Harland guard me every minute. However, to-night I went to bed early, and with Kalim's aid I was able to come here, but only on condition—the faithful Kalim determined to come with me."

"With you?" repeated Anastasia.

"He is hiding now in the distance of the garden," went on the Maharajah. "The darkness frightens him; he is fat, and short of breath."

He laughed a little, and, threading his arm through Anastasia's led her towards the grove of orange-trees.

"Rao," said Anastasia, "I have bad news. To-night my mother came to my room. She suspects us."

"She suspected us in London," said the Maharajah, "but in a few days, when I am restored, when these miscreants are cleared out from the palace, then I shall come to her in my true character, and ask her formally for your hand. You will give me that hand, little white flower of my soul?" he whispered passionately. As he spoke he raised her fingers to his lips.

"My hand and heart are yours already, Rao. I can hardly tell you what I have to say, but it means separation—it means—"

The Prince laughed softly.

"Can one," he asked, "separate the heart from the body?"

"You don't know my mother," said Anastasia. "You don't know how determined, how strong she is when she makes up her mind."

"Can her mind," asked the Prince, "make up your life? Can it give you love, or take love from you?"

Suddenly Anastasia turned towards him.

"I want you to understand," she said, "that I can't resist her. The day after to-morrow she is going to take me away. She would never consent to our marriage, I am certain of that; I have been certain of it all along. Often when I have wanted to confide in her, the thought of her implacable opposition to a marriage between us has held me back. Rao. I think she would rather see me dead than married to you!"

"To a 'Native,'" said the Maharajah, quietly. "She is like that, I understand. Cold and hard, and without understanding."

"But I love you," said the girl—"and the day after to-morrow I must go away!"

There was silence for a long minute. Night sounds came to them from the dreaming garden. Then the Prince spoke again.

"I can do nothing now," he said, "so long as I am in hiding. But in a few days Kathnagar will be mine again. You must not let your mother take you away. She cannot take you from me Anastasia. Rather than that," he said, suddenly, sitting up with his head erect—"rather than that, I would sacrifice everything! Kathnagar itself and all that Kathnagar means to me. Then would you and I mysteriously creep out together, and vanish from the eyes of the world."

He stopped suddenly. Power to love, and the power to express love, was inherent in him. The strangeness, the charm, the Western wonder of Anastasia's beauty had long evoked a love in his mind, which had grown to an over-powering passion. In the few minutes that they had been together he had forgotten that he was of the East and she of the West. When Anastasia had spoken of her mother's objection to the marriage, a sudden flare of contemptuous resentment at Lady Strickley's attitude had moved within him. But the idea that this insignificant woman of the West could object to him—to a Rajput of eight centuries of Royal birth—puzzled him, creating in his mind astonishment rather than anger.

"You understand, Anastasia, what I have said?"

"I understand, Rao."

"You must remain in Kathnagar until I am restored. Then I will ride in to see your mother, and make my demand. That is settled. But if she sets her will against yours, and makes it so that there is no escape, then we will do as I say."

He stopped abruptly, and clasped both hands in his.

"You will come with me secretly? You will not be afraid?"

Anastasia nodded her head slowly.

"I will come," she whispered. "I am afraid; but I trust you Rao. And you will be kind to me always, just as now? It is true, is it not, that a marriage between us could be happy—that you would not make me regret?"

The Maharaja did not answer, but in the light of the climbing moon, the burnished rim of which had risen above the purple-black trees at he edge of the garden, Anastasia read adoration in his eyes; and for a moment they remained face to face. The Prince's face drew nearer; something cool and soft floated down and settled on the back of Anastasia's hand.

"Rao, the petals, are falling," she whispered, and without knowledge of the cause a shudder went through her.

"Not yet," answered the Prince; "they are only now beginning to bloom."

A silence followed, and a low wailing noise, came to them.

"That is Kalim calling me," said the Prince. "He is either afraid, or he thinks I have been with you too long."

Anastasia rose suddenly to her feet.

"I had forgotten time, I had forgotten everything. I will send another message to you to-morrow, Rao."

"And you will not go?"

"I will not go."

"Then in a few days I will come and see your mother. When she understands, her answer will be less unkind."

"Now I must fly," whispered Anastasia. She had grown suddenly afraid.

21

The Plan of Attack

Carter had established several things in his mind. In the first place, a new enemy had arisen in the person of the sinister old woman who had examined the documents in the buhl cabinet some days before. This old woman was Gunara Tukaji, Sanquo's mother. He felt no doubt of that, for he had followed her zebu cart to the outskirts of Kathnagar and seen her enter the house.

He had waited and seen Sanquo ride up and enter the house, then subsequently ride away again. Another thing Carter had established in his own mind was the certainty that the House of the Silver Lily contained a secret entrance which, given leisure, it was his business to discover.

Recalling the three matches he had placed between the lintel and the door of Kalim's room, he decided that Kalim was a person to be trusted.

One night, a week after their arrival, Carter entered the drawing-room and found Taylor, Harland and the Maharajah in conversation. That is, Harland and the Maharaja talked, and Taylor listened with an air of supreme comprehension. They all turned as Carter entered, and the Maharajah rose from his chair and made a confession. Kalim had half recongised him, he said, and he had therefore revealed his identity to the fellow and told him something of the strange conspiracy which had placed Sanquo and Amoola Khan, the impostor, in the Palace of Kathnagar.

"You think it was unwise, indiscreet of me?" he asked, a little apprehensively.

"I think Kalim is to be trusted," answered Carter, quietly. "But as this house is not quite as impregnable as it might be, perhaps you'd close the door, Taylor."

Taylor closed the door and leaned with his back against it, and regarded Carter expectantly. The Maharajah, with the sensitive prescience of his race, paced the floor and watched Carter's face nervously.

"Harland knows my plan," said Carter. "We are here to replace your Highness at the Palace, and my instructions are that the work is to be done without the apparent intervention of the British authorities. When we arrived I thought we should be able to work slowly and lay our plans. I have changed my mind about that now," he went on decisively. "If your Highness is to be restored, it must be done to-night!"

He took a sheet of notepaper from his pocket, and, unfolding it, laid it upon the table. It was a plan, carefully pencilled from memory, of the first-floor apartments in the Palace of Kathnagar.

"Would your Highness kindly glance at this?" he said,

The Prince bent over the sheet of paper and scrutinised it for a minute.

"It is quite correct," he said, in answer to a further question of Carter's. He laid his pointed finger-nail on the centre of the plan. "That is my bedchamber," he said; "here is the long passage giving entrance to the zenana."

Carter spoke again in a much lower voice.

"Will your Highness tell me," he said, "if it is possible to get into that passage without disturbing the attendants?"

The Maharajah stroked his chin thoughtfully. Carter resumed: "I examined that passage carefully, and, if you will forgive me saying so, the lock on your Highness's door is a gimcrack, affair. Amoola Khan of course, occupies your bedchamber and your own State couch?"

"Yes," said the Maharajah; and he drew in a deep breath. For an instant his white teeth were visible. "The door of the State bedchamber," he said after a pause, "is never locked."

"That relieves us of one difficulty," said Carter, and he glanced at Harland, who had advanced to the desk and was examining the plan. "It is necessary," went on Carter, "for us to get to Amoola Khan without disturbing the Palace. Can your Highness suggest a way of doing that?"

"I am thinking," said the Prince, and he passed his hand slowly across his forehead.

"I have not yet been able to discover," went on Carter, "where Sanquo spends the night. But we shall find that out this evening during the Fête."

"On the west side of the Palace," said the Maharajah suddenly, "there is a narrow, iron-bound door, which leads up a narrow staircase into the zenana." He laid and indicative finger on a distant corner of Carter's map. "It is a door that is never used except by myself. That entrance, for hundreds of years, has been held sacred to the ruling Prince."

"You think it possible for us to get in that way?" questioned Carter quickly.

Captain Taylor, drawn by the interest of the situation, removed his back from the door and joined the group at the desk.

"Some years ago," said the Maharajah, "on my return from England, I had the door fitted with a combination lock. Unless Amoola Khan has changed that lock, you can get into the Palace that way."

He stopped, and looking up into Carter's face smiled rather oddly.

"Then," said Carter, interpreting that smile, "I suppose our troubles will begin."

"It might be possible," said the Maharajah, "for you to get through the outer passage of the zenana without disturbing the guard, but in the Palace itself are Pathans who never sleep. There are eight or ten of them on guard all night, and at intervals they patrol the passage outside the State bedchamber itself. There was always an armed Pathan on guard at the door from the moment I entered my room at night."

"That makes things a little awkward," said Carter. "Amoola Khan is sure to keep up that custom."

"Your Highness thinks it impossible to get to this fellow without arousing the Palace?" asked Harland.

"He'd fire his Snider instantly," said the Prince, "and the whole Palace would be in an uproar in a minute!"

"We must get this fellow from the door somehow," answered Carter, "and make our way into the State bed-chamber."

The Prince shook his head.

"It's impossible," he said.

"Harland and I are here to do it," said Carter brusquely, and began to pace the floor.

"Bribe him!" suggested Taylor, with a sudden flash of illumination.

"It would be impossible to bribe him with fifty elephants," said the Maharajah coldly. "He believes Amoola Khan to be myself!"

He spoke with an autocratic dignity and majesty that would have rebuffed anyone but a genial pachyderm such as Taylor. But Taylor, though he lacked ideas himself, had supplied Carter with one.

"Thanks," said Carter, "you've put me on the track."

"Why not get the Resident to arrest him?" said Taylor, elated by his success. "I don't like his wife, but Sir Boris himself is a decent sort of fellow."

"Quilliam describes him as a fool," said Carter.

"His daughter's a deuced pretty girl, anyway," said Taylor. "I saw her when I went to call on the old chap this morning."

The Prince's eyes lit up. He was thinking of the moonlit garden of the Residency when the faithful Kalim had kept watch for him.

Taylor alone had seen Sir Boris, and had made him acquainted with the extraordinary state of affairs and the secret plans for restoring the Maharajah.

"Don't talk," said Carter sharply, "you're not good at talking."

He drew the Maharajah aside.

"There is no way bribing this family of Pathans?"

The Maharajah shook his head.

"There is five hundred years of loyalty to us in their bones!"

"They are entirely without weakness?" questioned Harland.

"Hardly that." The Maharajah's teeth flashed in a smile.

Carter was thoughtful for a minute.

"I gather," he said, "that these fellows are entirely without likes and dislikes, and that their loyalty to you is their only marked characteristic!"

"That and a passion for jewellery," said the Maharajah.

Carter seized the point with the rapidity of lighting. He wearied the Maharajah with close, probing questions.

This loyal family of Pathans, he learned, were not fond of jewellery for its own sake, but there was rivalry among the younger members as to who could deck his wife in the greater number of gold anklets and jewelled bracelets.

"I understand, then," said Carter, at the end of the catechism, "that it is an invariable custom for a single armed Pathan to guard the door of the State bedroom?"

The Maharajah had already repeated this fact a number of times. He intimated as much to Carter, and smiled at Taylor who put in a word at that moment. Taylor, in addition to being bored, was inclined to be rebellious.

"I thought there was going to be a 'dust-up,'" he said, gloomily; "I'm like Harland. I came here solely on the chance of a 'dust-up'!"

He was a fine specimen of then unimaginative, valorous fool, who brings credit and honour to a regiment, and discredit and disaster to an army. In a situation such as the one that now presented itself he was entirely useless, but Carter knew that when it came to fighting he would be an asset of quite considerable importance.

"There is someone at the door," said Harland.

A low knock was repeated upon the panels, and Kalim presented himself. He salaamed low before the Maharajah, and advanced a step, or two into the room.

"What is it?" asked the Prince.

"Oh, Heaven-born," said Kalim, "it is exceeding presumptuous of this slave to make remark upon it, but"—he bowed low again—"but it is a quarter to seven."

Carter broke into a laugh.

"I see," he said, "you think we ought to be starting for the Palace."

Kalim bowed low again, and retreated backwards to the door. Carter followed him out of the room.

"You are a fairly wealthy man, Kalim?" he said in a pleasant voice.

Kalim raised his smooth brown hands deprecatingly.

"The Presence knows," he said, "that I am but a poor man. My poverty is a byword in Kathnagar."

"Therefore you would like a present of a hundred rupees?"

"If the Presence so desires it."

"You are to do a commission for me, Kalim. I wish to buy a bracelet—an expensive jewelled bracelet—one that will twinkle by lamplight."

Kalim smiled—something of the real man within penetrated his Eastern cuticle. He laid a short brown finger on Carter's waistcoat.

"I can lend the Presence a beautiful bracelet," he said, and a minute later Carter stepped back into the drawing-room. And thus it fell out that Kalim unwittingly helped forward Carter's great plan.

It was already seven o'clock, and Amoola Khan had invited

them to a small European dinner to be given in the Palace at eight.

When Carter and Taylor were ready to depart, and when a landau from the Palace was already waiting at the gate, Carter gripped the Maharajah's hand.

"Your Highness will be ready to come with us at half-past eleven?" he said.

The Maharajah, still holding his hand, assured him of this. "You think," he said in a low, hesitant voice, "all will go well?"

"I am sure of it!" replied Carter. "By this time to-morrow your Highness will be ruler again in Kathnagar."

When Carter and Taylor had driven away, Harland sat with the Maharajah for an hour in the drawing-room. Then he, too set out for the Fête. The Prince, who wanted to be alone, urged him to go, and, though Harland protested, he was at length obliged to submit. There was danger that by some mischance either Sanquo or Hajiz might recognise him; therefore by the Maharajah's advice he went forth in Native garments. Kalim provided these garments, which were the costume of the khitmagar.

In the House of the Silver lady there remained only Kalim and the Maharajah, and, obeying Carter's orders, Kalim carefully secured all the doors and windows of the building.

Kalim moved, soft-footed, from window to window, and door to door. The Maharajah's nerves were strung to the highest tension. He paced the floor of the drawing-room with his hands clenched and his head beat; minutes seemed to lengthen into hours.

He drew out his watch and glanced at the time. It was half-past nine—there were still two hours to wait! He knew that those two hours would be an eternity to him. He walked to the window and looked out into the night. His eyes involuntarily turned in the direction of the Palace, and he saw in the sky the glowing blood-red radiance of a Bengal light. In the shock of the first glance his heart turned to water—he feared the Palace was in flames. Then he understood—in his agitation he had forgotten the Fête. A spray of dazzling, coloured stars swept through the red light, and jewelled the sapphire sky for a moment, then a dull far-away report smote his ears.

For a full hour he stood there motionless. The red light became blue, and then green; other rockets jewelled the sky and died into blackness.

Meanwhile stout Kalim, in his little office, stood at a desk with a lamp beside him, and worked at his accounts.

"What's the time now?" called the Maharajah at length, opening the drawing-room door. He held his gold watch in his hand.

"It is half-past ten, O Heaven-born," said Kalim, and waited in the matted hall for further orders.

"Thank you," said the Prince. "I thought my watch was slow."

He retreated into the drawing-room, and closed the door quietly. Kalim waited a minute, in case his Royal master should reappear and desire to ask further questions. Then he returned to his accounts. It was noted afterwards how well he kept those accounts—what an excellent, loyal servant he was.

22

The Maharajah's Cigarette Case

Before the Palace stood a scarlet-covered dais, in the centre of which were two chairs of special significance. Sir Boris Strickley, the British Resident of Kathnagar, occupied one of these chairs, and upon the other was seated the slender, liquid-eyed impostor, Amoola Khan.

Behind Amoola Khan's chair, typifying his real position of the power behind the throne, stood Dr. Sanquo. At Amoola Khan's left hand was a vacant chair, behind which stood Carter, apparently in animated conversation with Sanquo.

Harland, in the khitmagar's costume, had from his station in the crowd watched for some time the distinguished guests seated before the Palace. The flare of the Bengal lights cast strange, glowing, fantastic shadows on the outlines of the Palace. Lurid gleams of flame seemed to leap and flicker in the five hundred windows. Sometimes the whole scene was bathed in an unearthly green light; again that light was blue, and more often red. Rockets boomed and leapt into the sky, expanding into naked, multi-coloured lights, and floated earthward.

Harland in his disguise had moved as near to Amoola Khan as was permitted to the undistinguished. He was near enough to see the expression on his face whenever a glare of light threw his brown features into relief. Somehow, Harland thoughts he saw fear in the depths of those melting black eyes. But perhaps that was merely imagination, for the fellow talked animatedly, and his white teeth gleamed as he smiled upon Sir Boris at his side. So far as the outward seeming of his part went, he played it to perfection. His costume was of the East, Eastern.

This was Harland's first view of Amoola Khan in his character of ruler of Kathnagar. He smiled grimly to himself when he recalled what that night might bring forth. In another hour or two he and Carter were to attempt to seize this glittering puppet, and thrust him back into the obscurity whence he had risen.

The word which opened the combination lock on the little door at the end of the Palace was "stealth." A perfectly fitting word. Harland thought, for the occasion. Carter had already assured himself that evening that the lock had not been changed, but Harland, moved by curiosity, worked his way round through the crowd to the western end of the Palace. He wanted to inspect that door for himself, and would have done so had not a tall Pathan in uniform seized him by the neck and aimed an energetic kick at him. Harland laughed to himself, dodged the kick, and moved away. The Pathan's attentions were, anyway, a testimony to the adequacy of his disguise.

Harland stepped in among the trees and became invisible A minute later Taylor appeared with two European ladies in white dresses. Harland was at that moment unable to make out more than vague, ghost-like outlines. He guessed, however, that they were members of the Resident's party—Lady Strickley, perhaps, and possibly Anastasia.

When the party had passed, Harland stepped from his hiding-place and followed at a distance. He was not at all pleased with the idea of revealing himself to English-women in his present guise, but he rather hankered for the company of Taylor. There was something in the British officer's good-homoured stupidity which was an attraction in itself. He was the kind of man one can sharpen one's wits on without fear of competition.

As Taylor and the two ladies came at length from beneath the shadow of the tiger-house, Harland stopped suddenly. His surmise was correct; the taller of the two women was Anastasia Strickley. He moved swiftly in an effort to overtake them, but they had already reached the outskirts of the Native crowd before he was able to reach them.

Taylor, with good-humoured masterfulness, was clearing a way for the elder lady who followed at his heels, and was in her turn followed by the girl. They were in the depths of the crowd when at length Harland laid his hand on Anastasia's sleeve.

"Miss Strickley," he said, in a low voice.

She turned and stared in utter amazement. Khitmagar's clothes, and the place they were in, conspired to create a complete disguise.

"I am Harland—Philip Harland."

She was looking into his face, in the lurid glow reflected from the Palace walls.

"I—I'm afraid I don't understand!" she said. "You—you are not a Native?"

Harland laughed, and in a moment she recognised him. His was a full-throated, hearty, infectious laugh, and it infected even the corners of Anastasia Strickley's finely curved lips. She glanced in the direction that Taylor and the elderly lady had taken; they were already lost in the crowd.

"Let me get you of this," said Harland briskly.

A few minutes later they were alone together, standing at the edge of the Versailles fountain, whose dancing spray reflected the garish lights of the fireworks, and became a plunging iridescence, the fragments of a shattered rainbow.

Harland looked into the girl's face. They had met but a few times in their lives, but they had already established an intimacy, an ease of manner towards each other. Anastasia questioned him as to his presence there, and his extraordinary get-up, but he was discretion itself.

"I don't exactly know why I am here," said Harland, in answer to her question. "Perhaps it is Fate."

They talked for several minutes, and Harland became gradually aware that the girl was subtly leading the conversation round to the subject of the Maharajah. His spirits sank; he had been inclined to forget that Anastasia was not interested in himself, but in the Prince.

In London he had been confident that she was in love with the Prince, and that the Maharajah was in love with her. Now, however, in the magic of the Eastern night, his egotism had caused him to forget that fact. He began to wonder again if the girl were deeply in love—if the Maharajah cared—and what would be the result of such an unfortunate state of affairs.

He knew that Lady Strickley would regard a marriage between her daughter and the Maharajah of Kathnagar in the light of a misfortune. Lady Strickley was a woman to whom the East was East, and the West was West, and Harland could guess that her soul would recoil in horror form the idea of such an alliance. Then he recalled Lady Strickley's exceptional affability towards himself in London, and it became apparent to his mind that Anastasia's mother had hoped that he might enter the lists as a rival to the Maharajah.

The idea that he could in any way rival the Prince struck him as preposterous. Nevertheless the night was propitious, and he did his best to charm and interest the exquisite girl who was seated on the edge of the fountain, and who talked to him with such frank friendliness.

Suddenly Anastasia rose to her feet.

"Mr. Harland, I must fly!" she said. "I shall be in terrible disgrace!" Then she turned and smiled at him, her face pallid, ethereal, and beautiful in the moonlight.

"But we have had," she said, "such a pleasant talk that I had forgotten all about the time."

Harland waited for a few minutes longer, then, following the last stragglers, made his way out of the Palace grounds, and on to the road. The hour must have been nearly eleven, and presently he heard the far-off jingle of an approaching carriage. He guessed Carter and Taylor were returning in a landau from the Palace.

He was now within a hundred yards of the House of the Silver Lily. There was something singular in its appearance. For a moment he was not quite sure what caused that singularity. Then he became conscious that it lay in the absence of light— no light shone from any of the windows. The drawing-room itself was in darkness.

The Maharajah's carriage bringing Carter and Taylor was already within hailing distance, and, as Carter alighted, Harland drew attention to the darkness of the house.

Carter's lips set in a tight line. The doubt that instantly leapt into his mind communicated itself to Harland, and in a measure penetrated Taylor's mind.

There was distinctly something wrong.

The Maharajah's carriage was dismissed, and the three men advanced up the garden path. Taylor beat heavily on the door with his sword-hilt. Faint echoes responded from the little coppice beyond the road, but no sound came from within the house.

They paused a minute, then Carter wrenched open a window to the left of the door, and Harland and Taylor followed him into the dark building. Harland struck a match, and by its fitful light they made their way into the hall which passed from the back to the front of the building.

Kalim's little office opened into the hall and its door was open. Something protruded from the doorway—a mountainous bloated something—which reached across the floor of the hall.

There was an awful, a tragic stillness in the house. Harland's match went out. He struck another, and in its first glare they saw that the mountainous thing was Kalim.

He was lying on his face, his feet still within the room of the little office. Under his left arm, and protruding from his side, was the bone handle of a heavy hunting-knife—the blade had been driven to the hilt in his flesh.

"My Gold!" cried Harland, "look at that!"

Taylor turned Kalim over, and raised him into a half-sitting position. He was quite dead; his eyes were open, and in the feeble light he stared at them strangely.

"The Maharajah!" gasped Taylor, looking up in wide-eyed horror.

But Carter, urged by the same dread, was already hurrying towards the Maharajah's bedroom. He found the door closed, and kicked it open—the Maharajah was not there! Then, followed by Harland, he hurried to the drawing-room. On the threshold he paused, and held up the lamp. The room was in the utmost disorder—the heavy buhl desk had been overturned, the lamp lay shattered on the floor, the oil making dark stains on the rush mats.

In the middle of the floor lay the Maharajah's gold cigarette-case, crushed and bent. The Maharajah himself had disappeared.

23

The Dark Hours

The awful silence of the house, the disordered drawing-room, the dead body of Kalim in the hall, and the absence of the Maharajah indicated something so appalling, so stupendous and catastrophic, that even Carter appeared to lose hope. The condition of the room pointed to a savage struggle. What the issue of that struggle had been they were at a loss to guess. But the Prince, whoever his assailants had been, had not surrendered easily. The situation appeared to be beyond words, and at length Harland moved softly into the room and picked up the Maharajah's battered cigarette-case.

He looked at it, then glanced at Carter. They were each busy with the outcome of that struggle. Was the Prince alive, or was he dead?

"If,' said Carter slowly, "they took the trouble to carry him off, there may be one chance in a hundred that he's still alive."

He was inspecting the outline of the case in the light of the lamp, and his eyes focused themselves on a horse-shoes of indentations which gave the impression of the teeth-marks of a strong man. For a moment he was at a loss to account for these marks; he thought they might have been made by a man biting the case in agony, or by the case being thrust into a man's mouth and forced upwards with great violence.

"What do you make of that?" he said to Harland, handing him the case.

"A man's boot-heel," answered Harland, with prompt practicality.

They were silent for a minute, for Carter's expression had changed. He was thinking quickly. Harland saw him clasp his hand unconsciously to his hip-pocket; he knew that his mind was busy; that he was master of himself again, and if the situation were to be dragged from disaster, even at the last moment, here was the man to do it.

They had forgotten Taylor; now his loud voice smoke their ears:

"Carter! Carter! Carter!"

And Carter leapt into the darkness of the hall like a man possessed. Taylor was still calling; he was in the bathroom adjoining the back bedroom of the house. When they reached him, he was on his hands and knees with a stump of candle in his hand, peering into a square black hole in the floor.

"What is it?"

"The way they took him out," said," said Taylor. "Here, hold the light; you can see a ladder."

Carter and Harland peered into the hole. A wooden trapdoor, usually covered by a mat, was flung back, and they saw, descending into the darkness, a narrow wooden ladder.

"I go first," said Taylor; "I found it."

Carter thrust him aside.

"Nobody goes," he said, "until I've examined it with the lamp."

Taylor was sent for the lamp from the little table in Kalim's office. It was necessary for him to step over Kalim's legs in making his journey.

"He looks horrible," he said, as he handed the lamp to Carter.

The trapdoor in the bathroom floor led to an underground passage some twenty yards in length, which the lamp showed to be empty.

"I think Harland's the man for this job," Carter; "he's got your nerve, and rather more than your brains."

Taylor remonstrated, but Harland was allowed to descend. He found the narrow passage dry and the air fresh. It ran in a straight line for twenty yards, then another ladder rose from the end wall. At Taylor's invitation he had accepted a Mauser pistol; this and the Colt in his hip-pocket made him feel like a walking arsenal.

Before ascending the ladder Harland glanced back, and in the feeble light of the lamp saw Taylor's inverted brown face looking at him enviously. There was a closed trapdoor above his head, he raised it softly, and found himself in utter darkness. A few minutes later he called Carter and Taylor, and they ran towards him along the passage, carrying the lamp. He had discovered that the passage opened into a store-room near the Native compound, and that one of the doors of this store-room was open.

On the red, sandy ground outside were the impressions of many footsteps. Among them was the impress of a man who wore heavy, heeled boots. Running straight from the door in parallel lines were two rail-like indentations.

"They took him out this way," said Carter; "those lines were the impress of his heels."

He held the lamp low, and for some minutes examined the numerous overlapping footsteps. Then he handed the lamp to Taylor, and bade him go back along the passage for all the cartridges he possessed.

When Taylor had disappeared down the trapdoor, Harland and Carter stood together in the silence and the ashy starlight. Carter had recovered his alertness and precision, but a subtle change appeared to have taken place in him. All his suavity, all his pleasant brightness of manner seems to have disappeared; when he spoke Harland read not only determination but a latent tone of ferocity in his words.

"Just one chance in a hundred!" he said; "this has been engineered by the old woman—I'd stake my reputation on that! She came in through the trapdoor the first night—that accounts for her fooling us when we watched outside! She and her emissaries came in through the trapdoor tonight. Kalim probably tried to raise the alarm, and they killed him—it was a strong man who drove that knife in his side. How the old devil discovered that the Prince was here is beyond me! But there's one thing pretty certain, the only chance of saving her son, and carrying on this seditious conspiracy of theirs, lies in the death of the Maharajah. That's why there's no time to waste!"

At that moment Taylor, bringing the cartridges, appeared like a genii, through the trapdoor in the storehouse.

"Now for the old woman," said Carter, when the cartridges had been shared among them. "Taylor," he said warningly, "when you see her, you must keep your eyes open—she's the toughest nut of this lot. We must get to her house and seize her—the Maharajah may be there."

The swift journey to the little house on the outskirts of Kathnagar occupied nearly half an hour. At length the three men stood before Gunara Tukaji's door, and Carter whispered his directions. The front of the place was in darkness, and he bade Taylor and Harland work their way round to the back, and conceal themselves in the garden.

"I'll bang at the front door," he said, "then if there's anybody particularly anxious to get away, they're sure to dash out at the back. I'll leave the rest to you."

Taylor and Harland proceeded at once to the back of the house, making stealthy progress from tree to tree. They arrived in the garden at last, and saw a low, blue light burning within the closed room in which Sanquo had interviewed his mother.

Tylor and Harland had been concealed in the garden little more than a minute, when the silence was broken by Carter banging at the front door of the house. Like a flash the blue light disappeared—the windows were flung open—and a man came leaping into the darkness.

Harland's fist caught him under the ear as he passed, and knocked him literally into Taylor's arms. He opened his mouth to bellow, and Taylor, in a dazzling flash of illumination, filled it with a handkerchief.

"If you make a sound," said Harland, speaking in the man's ear, "I'll blow your head off."

Carter was coming softly towards them.

"Bring him back into the room," he whispered, "he has evidently had a hand in the business, or he would not be so anxious to get away."

The fellow came unresistingly. A lamp was lit, and Hajiz, Sanquo's servant a Native dress and slippers, stood revealed to view. His eyes were wide open and watchful, but there was no fear in them; either he relied on the well-known clemency of the European, or he relied, on his capacity for tricking the European.

They made him seat himself on the divan, and Taylor stood over him with his Mauser.

"Don't let him make a noise," said Carter. "The old woman may be lurking in one of the rooms."

He passed out, and searched the little house from end to end. Clearly Hajiz was the only occupant. When Carter returned to the room he carried with him a heavy pair of army boots. He held them towards Hajiz.

"These are yours?" he asked.

Hajiz hesitated a minute—he was proud of those boots.

"Yes," he answered.

Carter drew up the wicker chair, in which Sanquo had that afternoon seated himself. He placed it so that he was directly opposite Hajiz—within a yard of him—then he rested a hand on each knee, and looked into the fellow's face.

"Close the widow, Harland," he said, without glancing round—and then to Hajiz "Where is the Native gentleman you took out of the House of the Silver Lily?"

Carter was too experienced to expect to read consternation or betrayal or any expression except duplicity on the fellow's face. Therefore, he was not surprised when Hajiz shook his head naively, and allowed a harmless, puzzled look to creep into his eyes.

"You don't know?" he repeated sharply.

"Not understand," said Hajiz.

Carter took from his pocket the gold cigarette-case.

"You trod on that to-night at the House of the Silver Lily," he said; "the man you captured there was His Highness the Maharajah. Myself, and these gentlemen, have been sent by the British Raj to protect His Highness."

He spoke with a smoothness which sounded almost polite but when he finished, he whipped out his revolver from his pocket, and added in a voice sharp as the rattle of musketry: "Now, you'll tell me where he is!"

Hajiz did not flinch; they were trying to get something out of him by pretending they would kill him. Of course they wouldn't do it. Your Sahib with a gold watch-chain, and probably a gold watch with bells in it, does not shoot Natives casually in a back room. The King-Emperor does not allow such things; he is apt even to hand the Sahib who does it over to the law.

Carter levelled the pistol at his head.

"I swear to you, Hajiz," he said, "in the presence of these gentlemen, that unless you answer my question in one minute I intend to pull this trigger! As a matter of formality" he added, "I will ask the consent of these gentlemen who will be witnesses of your execution. Do you consent?" he said, with a swift glance at Harland and Taylor. Perhaps there was a tail end of a wink in that glance, but it was unnoticed by Hajiz, who began to think things were taking an unpleasant turn. There was a pomposity and ceremony about the thing that gave it almost a judicial aspect. He began to wonder vaguely if he had unwittingly stumbled upon a court of justice. The ways of the Sahib are strange indeed. He felt something that can be better described as nothing—a vacuum in the pit of his stomach. His eyes, which appeared to have become suddenly all whites, travelled from face to face. There was the same set, strange implacability on the features of each of his adversaries.

"We consent!" said Harland and Taylor in duet.

Carter looked at Hajiz.

"Where is he?" he said, moving the barrel of his pistol a fraction of an inch. "Where is he?"

"I don't know!" The words in excellent English leapt from him in a last effort at duplicity.

Carter rose very solemnly.

"Gentlemen," he said, "you are witnesses to this——"

"No, no, no!" appealed Hajiz falling on his hands and knees and bowing his head to the floor. "He is in the Temple—the Temple of Vishnu. I know nothing; I see it quite by accident!"

"You trod on this cigarette-case by accident?" said Carter, with a grim smile towards Harland. "Now, get up, and take us to where he is."

Hajiz was a villain, possibly a murderer, but he possessed a swift instinct for keeping his own skin intact; moreover, Carter had succeeded in convincing him that his life was really in danger. If these three Sahibs were really sent by the British Raj, Sanquo would be overthrown. He wanted to be on the wining side, whichever side that might be; he felt that it was a little too early yet to decide, but in the meantime he became almost placable.

Carter, despite his air of calm, had been in mortal dread of what Hajiz might have to confess to him when his defences were at last broken down.

Was the Maharajah alive or was he dead? But it was here that Hajiz knowledge failed or appeared to fail him. The Prince had been conducted to the Temple by a company of soldiers from the Palace—of what had happened after that Hajiz swore he knew nothing. He was willing to accompany them and to show them the little gate which the Maharajah had entered, and that was all he could do—beyond that he knew nothing. That was all Carter could get out of him, and he was obliged to take the best of it.

A few minutes later the four men issued into the starlit road. Hajiz was placed under the charge of Taylor, who walked beside him; Carter and Harland followed. A rapid walk of ten minutes brought them to the outskirts of the great Temple of Vishnu. There were many small priestly buildings to pass before the Temple itself came into view, looking like a vast, yawning cavern, black as the mouth of Hades. It was after the hour of midnight, and the strange quality of the silence appeared to be as profound as death, and yet watchful.

The stupendous pile of carven sandstone blotted out the starlight, leaving these four little figures of men moving, as it were, in a pool of darkness.

Carter believed Hajiz, and he knew that somewhere within the walls of that brooding granite monster the man who had been given into his charge lay, a prisoner, and he was determined to rescue that prisoner in the teeth of all the priests in India.

The fact that the odds were against him—that the Prince might already have been made away with—that he and his friends might meet defeat and perhaps death, appeared merely to steady his nerves.

As they advanced softly in the darkness, even Taylor foresaw what he would have described as an "Al dust-up." Harland, with his old impetuosity, had outdistanced the others, and was already examining the Temple in search of a small door, which might either be open or lend itself to his persuasions.

They found the small door at last, but it was Carter's finesse which enabled them to finally gain access to the Temple. Carter was a paste-master in the art of making little keys to open big boxes, and his key, in this case, was a low whistle which issued from the lips of Taylor, who stood in the darkness ten yards away from the door in question. He stood directly in front of the door, and was placed there with strategic care by Carter.

Taylor whistled a second time, and a third, then the door opened softly, and an old, white-headed priest appeared in the dim light of the aperture. He had been disturbed in his devotions by that curious, unaccountable sound.

For a minute he stood in the doorway, peering before him, and saw nothing, then he made out the figures of Taylor and Hajiz. He moved forward to investigate, and Carter and Harland, who had been with flattened backs against the Temple wall, slipped into the building. The old priest, busy with his investigations, failed to notice their noiseless ingress.

"The Sahib wished to visit the Temple at that hour of the night?" He was talking to Taylor, now. "It was incredible. Impossible! The insanity of the Sahib in particular, of the British Raj in general, was undeniable—but this was beyond all utterance! Either this Sahib was moon-mad, or he was drunk with wine!" He turned his eyes to heaven and held aloft his hands. It was beyond his power; and outside the tenets of his high-thinking vocation, to be harsh, but he came very near to harshness in his urgent suggestions that the Sahib should choose a more reasonable hour for his visit.

Taylor was just the man to engage himself in a complicated and fatuous discussion of this sort, and he detained the priest there for ten valuable minutes.

In the meantime Carter and Harland, avoiding the votary lights, moved cautiously into the depths of the building.

24

The Disadvantages of
Being a Torchbearer

The low door which Hajiz had described as the one beyond which the Maharajah was imprisoned, stood at the far end of the Temple. Carter and Harland, moving in the monstrous shadows cast by enormous idols, made their way to it unobserved. A few old priests, engaged in trimming votary lights, flitted about in serene unconsciousness of the presence of unbelievers.

When at length they came to the broad, low door, they found it barred heavily and further secured with four long bolts. The business of slipping these bolts occupied interminable minutes, during any moment of which Harland expected to hear a squeal of discovery from one of the priests, but the door, giving a low groan, swung inward at last, and was closed behind them.

The stupendous, low-roofed, noisome place they had entered—the so-called stable and sanctuary of sacred animals—

was roofed with heavy, sweating granite blocks. In area it appeared to be vast beyond computation. There were regular aisles upon aisles of shining black marble gods—gods colossal and grotesque in tortured attitudes leering and smirking, and each with a multiplicity of arms radiating from the shoulders like the tentacles of an octopus.

For a few minutes Carter and Harland stood motionless, with backs to the low, closed door, striving to realise the extent of this terror-breeding wilderness of nightmares. So far as they could see, there were but three lights in the whole cavernous building, and each of these burned before a many-armed god, far down separate limitless avenues.

The air was warm, humid, and oppressive; the darkness was peculiar in that it appeared to be vaguely luminous and phosphorescent. Beneath their feet lay a yielding sodden dust, which was almost mud in consistency.

Harland whispered, breaking a long silence, during which their eyes had grown accustomed to the darkness. Carter turned, and looked at him.

"Can we risk calling him?" said Harland.

Carter shook his head.

At that moment a thin, squeaking cry pierce the close air, was repeated once, and again silence fell. Harland like a flash, flung his back against the wall again, and had his hand on his hip-pocket.

"Vampire bats," explained Carter. "The place is probably swarming with them." He touched Harland on the arm. "Let us explore the path in front of us."

They moved forward down a narrow avenue between scores of leering black gods placed at regular intervals. The idols reached almost to the granite roof, and were each sixteen or eighteen feet high. Making a cautious, silent progress forward, they glanced to the right and left, down endless other avenues peopled with similar monstrosities, but no sign of life met their eyes.

They reached the votary light at length, and Carter took it, a tiny glass bowl with a feeble, pulsating light, from its ledge amid garlands of dead flowers. Carrying the light, he advanced another hundred yards into the darkness, still between endless rows of idols. Suddenly their path was barred by the far wall of the chamber, a perspiring granite wall, with yellow fungus-like exudations lining the joints between its mighty blocks. They searched for a door in this wall, and at length found one, a small wooden door, scarcely five feet high, and three broad, almost opposite the door they had entered from the Temple.

Carter bent over the surface of the door carefully with his votary light, then pushed it gently inwards. It was locked. Something moved within.

"Is that your Highness?" whispered Harland in swift excitement.

There followed the rustle of straw, and then silence fell. A long silence, during which Carter and Harland did nothing, merely listened, waited, and hoped, without result.

A few minutes later Carter knocked softly four times, but no answer came from within. Then he put his lips close to the door, and spoke in a low voice.

"This is Carter your Highness!"

The straw rustled again, another pause followed; then a feeble voice came from within: "Speak again."

"This is Carter, your Highness, Carter speaking—Carter!"

"He's there, he's alive! Thank God for that!" cried Carter; then he turned to the door.

"Ah!" This last was a deep-drawn sigh from beyond the door. The Maharajah had recognised Carter's voice.

"Mr. Carter, can you do anything for me?" he whispered urgently. "I've been here for hours—hours!"

"We may be able to prise off the lock," returned Carter.

"Don't leave me!" came back the voice from behind the door.

The Maharajah was a courageous man, but either the horror of that cell or the horror of the night appeared to have unnerved him.

Nothing was said for a few minutes, during which Harland searched for something which might help them to prise off the heavy lock. He found nothing, although he made an extended excursion, peered along twenty or thirty narrow avenues, formed by the forest of idols.

When he returned to the low door he found Carter already there with a small block of granite just within the power of a man to lift. He had found this, together with half a dozen bags of cement, evidently placed there for the purpose of repairing the walls.

Later that night this same cement was, on two occasions, to do service in a good cause.

They could hear the Maharajah moving within his cell, and his urgent request that they should hurry came out to them in urgent whispers.

Carter began to hammer at the lock with his battering-ram of granite. In short, agitated sentences, the Maharajah told them, through the barred door, the story of Kalim's murder, and of his own capture and imprisonment. Hajiz and half-a-dozen others had crept in upon him as he stood in the drawing-room.

Carter was right; Sanquo's mother had led the way into the House of the Silver Lily, through the trapdoor in the bathroom. She had stood by during the Maharajah's struggle with Hajiz and two swarthy Pathans. She had begged these fellows to kill him, but they had refused to carry out her wishes without an order from the supposed Maharajah. He had been finally flung into that narrow hole of a cell, and the old woman, the Maharajah thought, had betaken herself to the Palace. When Carter first knocked on his prison door he confessed he thought his last hour had come. As Carter paused between the blows of the granite block, he learned that the rage of Gunara Tukaji had been terrible, and that she herself had made a rush at him with a knife when he was in the hands of the Pathans.

The lock began to show signs of giving. The perspiration streamed from Carter's forehead. The two feeble votary lights cast dim flickering beams upon the little door.

Harland, who had been staring away into the dark forest of idols, suddenly spoke, without turning his head; his words came swift and low.

"Do you hear that?"

Carter paused, and instantly blew out a light. There was but one light now in the whole vast cavernous area, and this burned on the marble slab at the knees of the god nearest the Maharajah's prison.

Carter dropped his piece of granite, took shelter behind the pedestal of this particular god, and waited. Footsteps were advancing along the avenue leading towards the Maharajah's place of confinement.

Other faint sounds in the distance caught their ears. Carter drew himself up, and peered cautiously over the granite pedestal, his eyes towards the long avenue of idols.

"I thought so," he whispered to Harland as he crouched again. Then he drew his Mauser pistol from his hip-pocket, and held it behind his back.

"Sanquo?" questioned Harland.

Carter nodded. "There is going to be a dust-up," he said under his breath, and smiled in the semi-darkness. The approaching footsteps drew nearer.

Cater suddenly deserted his ambuscade, and stepped into the open passage.

He had Sanquo were face to face.

Sanquo halted—he expressed no surprise.

"Very neatly arranged," he said, smiling cooly, with an insolent curl of the lip.

"You are a little earlier than I expected," retorted Carter, with equal coolness.

"I have wanted to meet you for a time," observed Sanquo. He glanced over Carter's shoulder, towards Harland, who now stood behind his friend. "Mr. Harland and you and I can settle our differences here without interruption. I owe the neat baiting of this trap to my mother. She is a wonderful woman, my mother."

"You are an excellent son." Carter smoothly. Then his voice rose, his tone altered. "You will understand, Sanquo, that I am here to remove you from your present sphere of action."

Sanquo turned his head. Like a flash he put out his hand and swept the only remaining light to the ground.

In the moment of complete darkness Carter fired.

The crack of his Mauser gave being to a hundred rolling echoes. The air of the vast, black cavern became alive with the beat and swish of wings, with the thin screams of startled bats.

"I'll make you pay for that," came Sanquo's voice from the darkness.

Harland promptly fired in the direction of his voice. They heard him moving again, and again his voice rose in a different place. This time he was further away, and shouted in Hindoostani. Carter and Harland moved, and, helping each other up, climbed to the pedestal of the nearest idol. Here, sheltering behind its stone arms, which made an efficient defensive screen, they saw a light suddenly flare up in the long aisle opposite the Maharajah's cell. The light, held aloft by a tall Pathan, smoked and glowed fitfully, revealing a group of dark-faced Natives in the uniform of the Maharajah's guard. The body of armed men—entirely filled the width of that particular aisle. The distance from Carter and Harland was something like forty yards, and Harland, watching from behind Buddha's long, protecting arms, saw Sanquo's face distinctly as he stood behind his men. Talking volubly at Sanquo's side stood a turbaned Native officer. At an order from the officer, the men levelled their rifles. Harland watched them in amazement. He followed the line of the rifle barrels with his eyes.

The rifles were directed at the door of the Maharajah's cell! The Native officer's high voice delivering an order rent the air.

"My God," said Carter, suddenly, "they're going to kill him through the door! Pick off the man with the torch!"

"Lie down, your Highness, lie down," called Carter in a low, penetrating voice.

He slipped from his pedestal, but Harland took aim where

he was, resting his hand on a stone wrist of Buddha. The next moment he fired. Sanquo's Pathan holding the torch flinched as if someone had pinched him, then opening his mouth wide, flung away his torch and ran yelling and leaping into the darkness. A great, daring looking fellow whiskered like a cat, bent forward and picked up the sputtering torch. Harland fired again, and he, too, dropped it. A comrade put an arm round him as he fell, and dragged him into the shelter of an idol.

Sanquo's riflemen lost formation, and began to back away uneasily. Harland saw the Doctor thrust them aside, and stamp the light out with his feet. In the darkness he fired at the spot, with the result which he fortunately had foreseen, for the flash of his Colt indicated his whereabouts, and a volley of rifle-shots chipped and mutilated the arms of his protecting idol.

"This is going to be a busy day," whispered Carter. "You are a marvellous shot, Harland. Save all your lead for the Doctor."

For a moment Harland entertained the idea of slipping down, and in among the body of riflemen. He badly wanted to get to grips with Sanquo. Sanquo had said that he and Carter were in a trap; for men in a trap they had managed up to that moment to give a very good account of themselves. He heard Carter whispering to him; "Harland, feel your way here near the Maharajah's cell."

Harland slipped from his pedestal, and groped towards the wall. He reached the cell, and Carter whispered to him.

"The Prince says the cell's too small to give him shelter— will get him if they fire at the door, rifle bullets will go through it like paper. We must get some of those bags of cement." He dragged Harland forward by the sleeve.

In the darkness they groped their way to the row of cement

bags, and in feverish haste each dragged a bag close up before the door.

"It needs at least three more," said Carter, "to just give him a chance."

They each made another journey, and each returned with a bag.

"Keep flat on your face," whispered Carter through the door, and dashed away for the fifth bag.

Scarcely three minutes had elapsed since the volley of shots had been fired at Harland, and whispered voices came to them from the surrounding darkness.

"What's his game?" whispered Harland.

"I don't know. We're out to protect the Maharajah, and—"

He never finished his sentence, for at that moment four flares of light quite near them sprang into simultaneous existence. Sanquo had cunningly divided his forces, and had disposed them so as to completely hem in his two opponents, for each torch-bearer was accompanied by two natives with rifles.

"The top of the idol!" called Carter, "it's our only chance!" and like a flash they both leapt upon the pedestal, and, climbing up the extended arms, crouched on the broad head of the god.

"Shoot the men with the lights," whispered Carter. "Never mind the others."

A torchbearer came into full view. Harland hit him and he danced a queer fandango to a screaming accompaniment. His torch fell to the ground, but no one picked it up.

25

Sanquo Limps in the Dark

arland's shot at the torchbearer had revealed their position, and there were still three lights moving warily forward, each backed by two gleaming rifle barrels.

A minute later one of these lights faded, and went out of it own accord. Carter guessed that Sanquo had been reduced to dividing his torch into four, and had so weakened its power. They were almost in darkness now, and the two remaining torchbearers seemed to have developed an intense affection for the shelter of distant idols. Sanquo's voice, calling an order in Hindoostani, resulted in a halt; and suddenly the two remaining lights, which had been glowing in the shelter of an idol, went out. Harland took a handkerchief from his pocket and wiped his forehead. The hot, damp atmosphere, and the excitement and activity of the last few minutes, made him feel particularly warm. He thought he heard a faint sound near the base of his idol— both he and Carter had been misled several times during the fight by the wild swooping of vampire bats—but this time Harland did hear something below him, and steadying himself by Carter's hand, he reached down and felt about in the darkness. His fingers came in gentle contact with the smooth barrel of a rifle aimed upward in his direction. He had just time to deflect its mouth when the man who held it fired. He was a brown figure stripped to the waist, and after firing he slipped away into the darkness like a lizard.

"A close call!" laughed Harland, preparing to follow him.

"Don't get down," whispered Carter, "the ground's alive with them, they intend to rush us in the dark."

Harland remained on the idol. For some minutes no sound broke the stillness save the soft clicking of Harland's Colt, as he slipped half-a-dozen fresh cartridges into place.

"I don't like this silence," went on Carter into Harland's ear. "It doesn't strike me as being particularly healthy! Sanquo's game may be to get rid of the Maharajah first, and attend to us afterwards. We must stop any attempt to get near the cell door."

In the distance busy whispering voices suddenly broke out, the patter of light footsteps, and the collected rattle of rifles. A sudden light fared in the long aisle, and Carter and Harland, looking down, saw the Maharajah's deluded soldiers present arms swiftly, and without a moment's hesitation fire at the door of the Maharajah's cell. The upper surface of the door was pitted with bullet holes, and as the rolling echoes died away a low, moaning cry issued from the interior of the cell.

"We must get some more bags of cement against the door," said Carter in a low, steady voice.

They slid from the idol. They light of the distant torch flickered on the low door, They had to pass that door, and the men were preparing to fire again.

Were they too late?

Harland wondered. Neither he nor Carter thought of themselves at that moment, though they carried their lives in their hands. They were putting forth a supreme effort to carry into effect the mission they had undertaken. They passed the door with whole skins, and returned, each carrying a bag of cement, which they placed upon the others as shelter for the prisoner within. The coolness and unexpectedness of the action saved their lives. Sanquo's men appeared to hesitate, and fired a fraction of a second too late.

Then the Maharajah, still miraculously alive, called through the door: "You can't help me." His voice was hoarse and low. "Save yourselves. I—thank you both." His words trailed away and became inaudible.

"I'm afraid he's right," whispered Carter. "They'll make a rush for the door now, and we can't keep twenty of them back."

The sudden, unpleasant things that had happened, however, had shaken Sanquo's men. There was a second's pause—he appeared to be exhorting them to something—to be commanding or threatening. Presently his voice ceased, and footsteps began to advance, softly along three of the avenues towards the Maharajah's cell. The Prince lay quiet now— ominously quiet, Harland thought. Sanquo had divided his force into three parties, and had left the torchbearer with his flaming light in the distance, evidently with instruction to keep himself under cover, but to hold his light so that its rays guided the men. The men themselves, advancing swiftly and almost noiselessly, were scarcely visible.

"We must do all the shooting we can," said Carter.

"We are easy marks up here," said Harland ruefully. "If they put a volley into us—"

"It looks like the end to me, too," said Carter.

He was lying flat on the idol with his Mauser ready, trying to watch the three aisles at once. The men came on rapidly, but it was too dark to see the angles of their rifles.

"You are right," whispered Harland, "they are making for the Maharaja's door. God help him! I would rather meet it here than there!"

Then the diversion of the night occurred. They heard a loud voice calling through the gloom.

"Hallo, you fellows! Where are you?"

It was Taylor's voice.

"Are you anywhere near the light?" shouted Carter joyously.

"I can see a fellow with a torch," said Taylor.

"Shoot him."

"Right-o!"

There followed an instant crack of a pistol, and the light went out.

"Thank God for that!" whispered Carter. "Now we can nip in among that lot down there, and give an account of ourselves.

"If we get out of this alive," whispered Harland to Carter. "I'll never laugh at a fool again."

"Who are these Pathans?" called Taylor again.

"They are Sanquo's lot." answered Harland. "Look out for yourself."

"Shall I try to get nearer you?" went on Taylor's voice through the darkness.

"No, Shoot at anything on your own level."

Almost instantly they heard the cracking of a pistol, fired rapidly, and the cry of a man in pain.

"We can't get down while he's doing that," laughed Harland.

Somehow it struck him as extremely amusing.

Carter and Harland clung to the top of their idol, and crouched there, watchful and alert.

Taylor's breezy intervention seemed to have given a new turn to affairs. There was silence for a time, then, a confused patter of feet. Harland had a vision of hurrying Native soldiers, and Taylor shooting in the direction of the slightest noise.

"Hallo, Taylor!" called Carter.

"Hallo!"

He was much nearer now.

"The next time the light goes up pick off Sanquo!"

"Right!" answered Taylor cheerily.

But he failed to pick off Sanquo, who had dispatched two of his men, who fell on their hands and knees and crept among the idols, seeking to take Taylor in the rear.

Taylor, however, was a natural soldier; he had no idea of remaining in the place where he had last spoken. He moved warily in short rushes towards the spot whence Carter's voice had come to him, and in his progress among the idols he came upon a whispered colloquy. Sanquo was there in the darkness, haranguing his gathering men in Hindoostani. Taylor heard him insisting that someone should hold the light. He heard him instructing that unseen someone how he was to take cover between the idols.

Taylor crept nearer. This was one of the moments of his life. He waited for the match which would illuminate the party when the torch was lit, and the moment Sanquo struck it he fired at him. But Sanquo was partly shielded by the Native officer; the bullet grazed the man's arm.

Sanquo's match had gone out, but in the darkness he seized

a rifle, and fired at Taylor without taking aim. Taylor uttered a curious exclamation of surprise. Then, in ungovernable rage, Sanquo thrust aside his men and sprang at Taylor. This was a tactical mistake, for the man he grappled in the darkness was not Taylor, but Harland who had crept stealthily along the avenue, and was within five yards of Sanquo when he struck the match. Sanquo's Pathans were puzzled beyond measure at the disconcerting ebb and flow of events.

They wavered, and whispered rapidly, together, and at that moment a loud parade-ground voice rattled out an order in Hindoostani, repeated that order a second time, and drove it home with a third repetition.

Taylor had achieved a master stroke of strategy.

Taylor's order for dispersal had scarcely left his lips, when the soldiers began to retreat slowly, to disperse and make soft tracks for the little door leading to the Temple.

The Native officer drew his sword and screamed out high-pitched voluble words; but the men were already on the verge of panic. They had received an order to disperse, and they meant to obey it. Whether that order were genuine or not mattered little to them at the moment, but it managed to jump with their inclinations; and, at any rate, the place was too full of surprises, too full of active men who shot at your from behind marble gods the moment you held up a light.

Therefore, the high-nosed, sword-waving Native gentleman screamed in vain. The distant door into the Temple opened, and a stream of hurrying men passed through it.

There was an odd, mixed-up struggle proceeding on the ground. Harland had seized Sanquo's wrists, and he meant to keep his grip on them.

Taylor, using his left leg, hopped along towards Sanquo and Harland. He presented his empty Mauser at Sanquo's head, and in the light of the little lamp called him to surrender. And that ineffable scoundrel, after a minute's pause—during which, no doubt, he thought unutterable things—gave in, or pretended to give in.

"I managed to break your leg!" he said, with a malicious glance at Taylor, as he rose to his feet, and shook the dust from himself.

"I managed to disperse your men," retorted Taylor, "so we are pretty well quits!"

Harland stood behind Sanquo, holding him by the collar. Sanquo turned and glanced over his shoulder.

"That impostor of yours is dead!" he said.

At that moment Carter, who had lit a votary lamp, reached them.

The Native officer had followed his men through the little door into the temple, and Sanquo, the last of the enemy, was apparently at the end of his tether.

"Things didn't fall out quite as you expected," said Carter to Sanquo, between his teeth. "Hold up his hands, Harland. He's probably got the key of the cell."

"He thinks he's killed the Maharajah," said Taylor.

Carter found the big key in the pocket of Sanquo's dinner-jacket.

"The man we shot through the cell door," said Sanquo, with the utmost coolness, "was an impostor. I am here at the order of the Maharajah himself. The Maharajah will know how to deal with you!"

A sound issued from Taylor's lips which was either a laugh

or a groan. He appeared to be swaying a little. Harland moved towards him in unconscious sympathy, and Sanquo seized the moment to slip dexterously out of his coat dash out the only light and disappear down the long avenue.

"We mustn't lose him now!" cried Carter, leaping after him. "Get to the Temple door, Harland; there's only one way out."

They were obliged to leave Taylor.

"Don't mind me," said Taylor, as Harland ran to take his station at the door. "I'll have a shot a him if he comes within range."

He hopped into the avenue, and groped about for the fallen light; but he was without matches, and the pain of his injured leg had become an agony. He subsided on to the ground, and remained there with his back against the granite plinth. Beads of perspiration arose upon his forehead. He was quite happy, however—he had participated in a dust-up, really an Al dust-up—and what more could a man want?

Carter had matches in his pocket, but, without striking a light, he followed Sanquo's retreating footsteps warily. He was conscious that the supreme test of his ability was at hand. What had been a general engagement had concentrated into a duel. It was now his subtlety and audacity against the cunning and enterprise of the cleverest scoundrel he had ever met. His ears were good; he could detect Sanquo's position by his moving footsteps, and coming to a standstill in the darkness he levelled his barrel in the direction of the sound, and fired. Sanquo uttered a low cry, and began to move more slowly.

Carter halted and listened; the Doctor's footsteps were irregular and halting. He was either wounded or pretending to be wounded—for he walked slowly, and with a limp. Carter followed in the intense darkness, groping his way forward with a hand on the clammy wall; he was overtaking Sanquo rapidly. The Doctor ceased to advance, and Carter heard a click, then a muttered exclamation. Sanquo had used his last cartridge.

Carter moved warily forward, still using granite pedestals as cover.

"It's all up, Sanquo," he said.

"You haven't got me yet," called Sanquo; and again Carter heard those halting footsteps, rather faster now.

This quickening of Sanquo's speed raised a faint doubt in Carter. He wondered what was taking place in that evil, scheming mind. This was no time for taking chances. Something brushed against his leg. He leapt away, then laughed to himself. He had come across another row of cement bags!

Sanquo's footsteps ceased altogether.

A strange creaking noise came to Carter's ears from the spot where the Doctor appeared to have halted, but always the moment Carter began to move, those limping footsteps began again. Sanquo was either seriously, wounded or—How did he know that click represented Sanquo's last cartridge, and what was that peculiar creaking which appeared to issued from the ground? Carter halted, then moved again in pursuit, for Sanquo's footsteps had begun again—very slowly now. Carter, as he advanced, put forward each foot suspiciously—rather in the manner of an elephant crossing a bridge.

He had advanced in this fashion some fifteen feet, when a sudden thrill went through him.

No ground met his descending foot—he had halted on the verge of a chasm!

Very softly he went down on his knees, and felt about with

his hands. There was a cavity in the ground before him, which extended half-way across the passage, and evidently had been covered by a trap-door. In the utter darkness the depth of the cavity was beyond his knowledge. Sanquo had not descended through that trap-door, for his halting footsteps still sounded ahead, invitingly drawing Carter onward. In a flash Carter understood everything.

He was being lured forward to walk into that chasm!

The subtlety and diabolical ingenuity of the trick made him catch his breath.

For a long minute he remained there motionless; then his own ingenuity came to his aid. He moved to the wall, took up a bag of cement, held it over the cavity, and dropped it into space.

For a moment there was silence then a loud splash sounded through the dark passage, and a reek of brackish water came up to him.

He was waiting for Sanquo's next move, and it came. In an instant he heard running footsteps advancing swiftly towards him. Sanquo, no longer lame, halted scarcely ten feet away. Carter felt he could almost reach him across the chasm. Then a puff of evil-smelling air blew in his face. The trap-door crashed shut.

Sanquo uttered a loud cry of unrestrained exultation, and leapt upon it. Then something sprang out of the darkness, and hurled him backwards to the ground. Carter's strong hands tightened about his throat.

26

Something Comes in at a Window

Carter, remembering Sanquo's dexterous escape from Harland, was not in the mood for taking chances. That Sanquo had been motionless for two minutes foretold nothing of what he would do, if given fraction of an opportunity.

Raising his voice he called to Harland, who was standing at the distant door of the Temple. Taylor took up his calls, and passed the word along for a light. And presently Harland, who had taken a light from the Temple, wound his way in and out among the idols, and drew up at Carter's side. The feeble light feel on Sanquo's upturned yellow face. His eyes were closed, and his lips tightly pressed together; there was perspiration on his brow, and the veins of his temple were distended. He was in white shirtsleeves, smeared and blackened.

Carter bade Harland put the light out of his reach, and go through him in quest of a hidden weapon. They found nothing upon him, however.

Someone moved in the distance, and by the feeble light they saw Taylor hopping laboriously towards them. Whether his insatiable appetite for a dust-up, or his desire to be in at the death, caused him to take the agonising journey was not apparent, but when he reached them he collapsed upon a bag of cement, and breathed heavily.

"Got—a—game—leg," he said, in jerky explanation of a wry face and a convulsive clenching of his hands. Then, white to the lips, he smiled pleasantly, and leaned against the damp granite wall.

Sanquo opened his eyes and looked at him; he appeared about to speak, and moved his lips, but merely moistened them with his tongue and lay still. Carter had risen and stood over him, his Mauser in his hand. He was in a fever to get to the Maharajah in his cell, and he handed his pistol to Harland. Then, leaving Sanquo in his and Taylor's charge, he hurried away down the passage. Harland, with a pistol in his hand and a watchful and relentless eye on Sanquo, held aloft the light, so that its radiance should reach Carter as he went.

Carter reached the damaged cell door, and Harland saw him bend low and insert the heavy key in the lock. Carter confessed afterwards that that moment was quite the shakiest in his life. He spoke through he door as he put the key in, but no answer came from within. He pushed it open, and felt about with his hands—the Maharajah was lying on the straw-covered floor, motionless and inert.

Carter placed his arms about him, and came out into the passage with him.

The Maharajah's head hung back limply—there was a welter of blood on his white shirt, and his eyes were closed. Carter laid him gently down on the yielding black dust of the passage; then striding along to Sanquo with a ferocity that startled even Harland, seized him by the shirt-front and wrenched him to his feet. At that moment he hoped with all his heart that Sanquo would again try to escape, in which case he would have lived possibly half a minute.

Harland and he conducted Sanquo down the passage with a pistol at his back, and flung him into the Maharajah's cell. The shot-perforated door was still sound enough to hold a prisoner. But even when the heavy key had been turned in the lock, Carter was not satisfied, and the indomitable Taylor volunteered another agnosing, hopping journey, and seated himself, Mauser in hand, on the little barricade of cement bags outside the cell door.

In the meantime Carter examined the wounded man slowly and carefully. His clothes were in tatters, and the great dark stain of blood began at the shoulder of his shirt and extended down its front. Harland held aloft the little glass-shielded light, and as Carter sought the wound, the Maharajah opened his eyes slowly, and turned them upon him.

For a minute he stared as one in a dream, then the light of recognition arose in them. He held out a thin, brown hand, and clasped Carter's hand feverishly. For a moment they remained thus, but there was his wound to consider—a rifle bullet had struck the side of his neck—had furrowed a line in the flesh. It was an ugly wound, but there was no danger in it, though it bled freely. They bound it about with handkerchiefs, and the Maharajah closed his eyes again. Once or twice, as Carter knelt supporting him, the Prince shuddered slightly.

"We must get him into the air," said Carter.

27

The.Power behind the Throne

n the night of the Fête, during the hours when the
Maharajah suffered his agony, and the duel of wits took
place between Sanquo and Carter, a bent, white figure
 desk in an inner room of the Palace of Kathnagar.
nara Tukaji was at work.

e who is the centre and heart of a vast conspiracy can find
isure for tranquil contemplation. The room in which she
s small and heavily furnished in the Western fashion. In
iddle of the apartment was a heavy board-room table
d with swivel chairs; on the wall above Gunara's desk hung
 big-figured calendar; and the top of the desk itself was
ied by an up-to-date Western clock, which lacked a face,
nveyed the time minute by minute with the aid of flicking
gles of cardboard. On either side of this clock were
rd electric lamps with flexible brass stems, which allowed
ght to be concentrated in any direction. The floor of the
was carpeted with a deep, rich pile carpet of a practical

The Prince was a small-boned man, and Carter lifted him
easily. Harland followed, holding the light. They reached the
little door leading to the outer Temple at length. Both Carter
and Harland expected trouble when they stepped into the
Temple, but the building was as silent as the grave. The
Maharajah, lying in Carter's arms, remained unconscious until
they reached the garden of the House of the Silver Lily. Then
he opened his eyes and uttered a half-conscious cry of horror.

"It's all right," said Carter, "it's all right."

Harland went in at the window, and opened the green
wooden door. He had gone first by tacit consent, as there was
an unpleasant duty to perform before the Maharajah was
brought into the house. It was necessary for him to drag Kalim's
heavy body across the passage, and close the little door of his
office upon it.

They carried the Maharajah into the drawing-room, and laid
him in the long wicker chair.

During the time Carter attended to the Prince in the drawing-
room, Harland had slipped away and despatched one of the
Native servants from the compound into Kathnagar with a chit,
telling the doctor there to go to Taylor's aid.

The Maharajah had now recovered sufficiently to sit up and
drink a whiskey-and soda with some degree of tranquillity.

"We have that fellow in safe keeping at last," said the Prince,
referring to Sanquo. "To-night is the time to act."

Carter was quiet for a few minutes, staring towards the silver
moon, which had risen suddenly, keen as a scimitar blade above
the tree-tops.

"That is true, your Highness," he said at last. "Sanquo is laid
by the heels, but there is still Gunara Tukaji. It was she, and not

Sanquo, who engineered your capture. A woman who is capable of that piece of swift villainy is capable of anything!" He came into the room and poured himself out a peg of whiskey. "We must keep our eyes open for Sanquo's mother," he added as he drank.

Harland, seated in a wicker chair, luxuriously smoking an excellent cigar, had been quite unconsciously watching the Maharajah's face. Carter and he had saved the Maharajah's life, but the Prince had made no mention of that fact since their return to the House of the Silver Lily. At first, and before he had fully recovered, he had shown a disposition to cling to Carter as though for protection. Now it seemed for a while as though his impatience made him the leader of the company. He was manifestly eager to be away—manifestly eager to bring to a climax the drama of his reinstatement. Harland admired his spirit wholeheartedly, but one thing struck him as curious and unpleasant—the look in the Maharajah's eyes each time that Sanquo or Sanquo's mother was mentioned.

"When shall we go to the Palace?" asked the Maharajah suddenly.

"We'll go now," said Carter, "and by this time to-morrow—" he held up his glass; Harland and the Maharajah each took up a glass. For the moment the three stood together in the quiet room; the three glasses were upraised.

"To the success of to-night and to-morrow!" said Carter; the glasses clinked, and at that moment there came to their ears a soft whirring sound, like the wounded flapping of a heavy bird. Something white entered the window, and bounding to the floor rolled clumsily in an irregular circle, and grew still.

Harland sprang forward and picked it up. It was a reed-pith helmet, battered and stained, and there was a bullet-hole

through it, from front to back. All t[...] Harland's face as he looked at it.

It was Taylor's helmet—and the b[...] down through the brim at the front, and [...] brim at the back. Carter leapt on to [...] profound silence brooded over the moo[...]

THE POWER BEHIND THE THRONE   **183**

colour, a carpet that would have appealed to the fancy of a Hebrew financier.

Gunara Tukaji worked until the clock showed the hour of one. Then she put down her pen, and leaned back in the swivel chair. She made a strange figure in that room, that might have been the Throgmorton Street office of a Hebrew financier. Suddenly she chapped her lean, dark hands together loudly, and in swift answer to her summons, a dark-skinned servant appeared on the threshold. Gunara glanced at him keenly.

"My son has not returned?" she inquired.

The man informed her submissively that Sanquo had not returned, and Gunara dismissed him with a wave of her hand. A moment later she drew down the roll-top of the desk, and glided out of the room. In her ornate heelless slippers she moved almost without sound along the broad marble-paved passage. At length she came to an iron-studded door, which she pushed open. Beyond the door was a flight of black marble steps, which descended to yet another passage, this time an underground passage entirely without ornament, and illuminated only by a row of plain electric bulbs depending from the ceiling. Waiting at the foot of the steps was a servant in the Maharajah's uniform.

Gunara, in curt phrases, ordered him to bar and close the door by which she had entered; then, taking no further notice of the man, proceeded along the passage to a door even more massive than the one at the head of the stairs. There was a minute's pause, and the door was drawn open—Gunara Tukaji stepped forward into the vaults of the Palace.

An electric fan whirred softly at the far end of the vault, and the place itself was brilliantly illuminated with naked electric lights. A dozen men were energetically at work in the business of sedition, for what had been the Maharajah's jewel vaults had been converted by Gunara Tukaji into a printing office for the production of a newspaper.

It was for the purpose of discovering a perfectly secure place of production for this newspaper that Gunara Tukaji had formulated her dazzling scheme. It was for the purpose of protecting her newspaper and pamphlets from the Indian authorities that she had virtually seized the principality and the Palace of Kathnagar. She knew, in that fathomless mind of hers, that nothing could serve her purpose of sedition so well as a widely circulated newspaper that was not subject to periodical suspension. She and Sanquo had produced newspapers before in different parts of India. A little harm had been done, some impression had been made on the minds of fanatical young Natives, but the police had always discovered the printing-presses at the critical moment.

With these past disasters in her mind, Gunara Takaji had set her keen wits to work, and had hit upon the daring coup of her life—the idea of substituting a tool of her own for a loyal and reigning prince. Sanquo had worked well in this matter. Amoola Khan had also done his share, and as Gunara Tukaji swept the scene before her with keen eyes, she smiled with inward satisfaction at the thought that she had so well succeeded where others had failed.

Two men had advanced towards her as the vault door closed. One of them was a sleek, round-faced babu, with large spectacles and a senatorial manner. He spoke generally, and at large, with the pomposity of his kind, and invariably when opportunity arose he spoke in English.

"You come," he said, "at psychological moment. Paper is

now upon press." He waved his hand towards the printing-press, which occupied the further end of the room.

Two Natives stood at the press, waiting for the order to start printing. Two other men stood, each with a flat stick of wood in his hand, at a smooth wooden bench—these were the folders who took the papers from the old-fashioned press, folded, cut, and counted them. In careful piles near the press were heavy packets of paper. Here, also, stood a man waiting to feed the paper into the press.

"With you permission," went on the babu, "we will proceed."

Gunara nodded curtly, and the babu, with a ceremonial air, strode away.

"Commence," he said, and simultaneously the hand-press began to move.

Gunara Tukaji turned to the other man who had come to her side when she entered the room. This was a little wizened man with black, shining eyes, a high forehead, and a peaked chin. He was a thin, gnarled old man, whose hands had grown horny with toil.

"Raheem", she said "you carried out my orders?"

Raheem rubbed his hard hands together, and smiled brightly.

"Everything goes well," he said. "There is much question as to where our papers come from. The police are paying bribes, but our plan of distribution has not been suspected."

"It is not of that I ask," said Gunara in her sharp voice. "What of to-night? You tell me that the mem-sahib is about to go away, and is to take her daughter with her. What signs are there that she is going to do this in truth?"

"I crave your forgiveness for forgetting, but this work of ours burns in my brain like a never-dying fire! The mem-sahib, she is going away truly; everything is ready; the boxes are packed; letters have been written."

"And the young feringhee woman?" broke in Gunara. "Have there been any more meetings in the garden?"

"There have been none," responded the old man. "I have seen none."

Gunara Tukaji suddenly turned, and looked down into his face.

"Remember, Raheem, it is wise that we should watch these memlog. Danger may lie there for our cause; we must know all that takes place. You have done well, Raheem. When the great day comes, you will not be forgotten!"

Suddenly Gunara lowered her voice.

"Raheem," she asked, "what news is there for my ear alone?"

"There is no news," answered the old man. "All flows smoothly as gentle waters in the long valleys. Among thy servants there is no thought but of the cause. There is no wavering, there is no thought of self."

For a moment Gunara Tukaji looked at him. Then she turned away, and moved towards the door. As she went she muttered a low-toned invocation.

Raheem leapt towards the closed door, drew back the bolts, and held it open for her to pass out. Gunara passed along the underground passage, and up the marble steps; there again a man drew open the door, and closed it behind her. Once more she was in the long Moorish corridor of the Palace itself. The corridor was deserted, and as Gunara walked forward in her slippered feet, her mind worked rapidly. She continued her walk until she reached the heavy ornate screens which shielded the entrance to the zenana. Here she halted, and listened.

A faint strumming, the low throb of a tom-tom came to her.

She paused a moment, listening; then, slipping aside a curtain, entered a dark, narrow passage, ascended a few steps, and peered through an ornate lattice-work of delicately carved marble, marble chiselled almost to the fragility of lace. Here she stood almost in entire darkness, peering through the carved stone trellis-work into a room below.

The room was illuminated by a crystal chandelier which hung from the ceiling. Against the further wall stood a dais and a sofa of chiselled silver strewn with thick cushions. On the sofa, reclining in sublime magnificence, was Amoola Khan. He still wore his turban and his tabard of green silk lined with purple satin; his muslin scarf was still about his neck.

28

Raheem's Mission

Gunara watched Amoola Khan unseen from behind the stone lattice-work. It pleased her to think of him as her handiwork. It was her mind that had engineered that magnificent imposture; it was at her bidding that he posed so superbly, assuming the *rôle* of the true Prince whom he had replaced. Perhaps in his own mind he had already begun to believe himself the real monarch of Kathnagar. She felt that she had built well in these past few months; everything had moved according to her desire. True there had been checks and set-backs. That was inevitable; he who climbs high, must of necessity, slip a little in the ascent.

There had been her son Sanquo's mistake in London, when he had permitted the rescue of the Maharajah. That had been a grave mistake, and one likely to have wrought serious consequences. Then again there had been her own mistake in not seeing through the mission headed by Taylor and Carter, which had come to Kathnagar. Nevertheless it was she who had doubted Harland, the man who had accompanied that mission. The fact that Harland's dressing case was equal in quality with that of his supposed master, had revealed to Sanquo that the mission to Kathnagar was not so innocent as it appeared.

For a few hours after that she thought that she had under-estimated the power of the British Raj. Then her indomitable spirit had risen again. Even the discovery of the fact that the real Maharajah of Kathnagar was in hiding in the House of the Silver Lily, the fact that the mission, headed by Taylor and Carter, was really in Kathnagar for the restoration of the Maharajah secretly to his own position, had not dashed her courage.

She had made plans, swift and merciless plans, which it behoved Sanquo to carry out without error. To-night great work was toward in Kathnagar; the final act of the drama she had played since girlhood was sweeping to its close. She permitted no thought of failure to find its way into her mind. The secret passage leading into the House of the Silver Lily, the passage she had used when she examined Taylor's letters on the first night of their arrival, had been used again. This time, the Maharajah was to be dealt with finally. What was one life when the whole of India must some day rise at her bidding?

She became conscious of a growing restlessness; she could no longer remain seated in the dark room behind the stonework. Sanquo, who had been despatched to the Temple of Vishnu to see that her bidding had been carried into effect, was almost due to return. She moved towards the office which she had left earlier in the evening; she had told Sanquo she would wait for him there. It was there she was to receive the news of the consummation of her plans, of the death of the Maharajah in his cell in the Temple. After that no power on earth could prove that Amoola Khan was an impostor. Only herself and her son knew his secret.

The situation was magnificent in its simplicity.

When at length she reached the door of the room, she found it ajar and a light burning within. She had moved forward noiselessly. Now she halted, listening, and a sound of heavy breathing beyond the half-open door stirred the silence.

Gunara's hands clenched suddenly together, a hard light blazed in her eyes. With the stealth of a serpent she glided into the room.

Hajiz was there, leaning against the board-room table. He was breathing heavily, there was a look of terror in his eyes, and he was winding his puggaree with a shaking hand.

Gunara Takaji drew the curtain behind her, then waited with her back against it, and her eagle eyes fixed upon Hajiz's face.

Hajiz lowered his hand from his turban.

"O mother of men," he panted, "many thing have happened. I have come to you with the speed of the wind, and I am afraid."

Gunara moved a pace or two towards him.

"Where is my son?"

She uttered the words in low, quelling voice, and she saw Hajiz flinch away as though a whip had struck his face.

"Where is my son?" repeated Gunara.

"He is in the hands of the Gora-log," answered Hajiz shakingly. "We made a good fight, O mother of men, but they were aided by devils. First they seized me and dragged me to the Sanctuary of the Gods, swearing I should die there because of my loyalty to you; when in the darkness I slipped away they had already captured that great one, your son. He is now in their hands, bound hand and foot."

Gunara Tukaji raised her hands; her face was as a bronze mask, but the glowing eyes raked Hajiz's soul. In that moment she realized that the Cause was more to her than even the life or death of her son.

"Where is that other one," she asked—"he whom you took from the House of the Silver Lily?"

Hajiz raised his head.

"Of this there is no doubt," he said, "that one is dead within the cell, for before the sahib could lay hands on thy son and those who came with him, the Maharajah's solders poured in a volley upon the prisoner."

"You are sure of this?"

Hajiz swore a great oath by all his gods. Gunara Tukaji peered deep into his eyes, but even she could not window lies from truth. Possibly Hajiz himself was not aware what part of this story was true, what part was bred of a heated imagination, and what part was invented to placate this terrible hawk-eyed woman who stared deep into his soul, making him feel transparent as the air.

"You are sure that one is dead?"

Hajiz swore again that doubt the Maharajah had been killed in his cell. Then Gunara Tukaji's mind leapt back to her son. They were within the dominions of the Maharajah—from now henceforth Amoola Khan ruled in Kathnagar. That is, Amoola Khan wore all the trappings of office, and she, Gunara Tukaji, wielded all power through him! Sanquo's capture by Taylor and Carter was an unfortunate accident, but there was still time to right things in regard to her son.

For a minute she remained with her head bowed deep in thought, and Hajiz stood at attention waiting for orders.

Suddenly Gunara Tukaji raised her hands and clapped loudly, once, twice, thrice. There was a pause, then a servant came running.

Five minutes later, in answer to her summons, a subordinate officer of the Maharajah's guard appeared before her, and in the presence of Hajiz she gave directions.

"You will send out," she said, "a body of men not in uniform. They are to attack those who hold my son prisoner. He is to be released. As the men attack they are to cry out that the Temple of Vishnu has been desecrated; they are to call out for vengeance to the gods! In no way must these men be associated with the Palace, but one thing alone must be accomplished—my son must be rescued."

Suddenly she paused abruptly.

"These are the Maharajah's orders," she said. "Hajiz will give you all knowledge as to where my son is to be found. Remember," she added warningly, as the officer strode to the door—"remember there is to be no mistake!"

A minute later she was alone in the room. Her ruthless, clear mind worked swiftly. Again she clapped her hands.

"I would see Raheem here at once," she said to the servant who had presented himself.

For five minutes she waited for Raheem, the gnarled old gardener. She had sent men to rescue Sanquo, but there still might be a mistake, therefore there was one other card which she might play. She knew, through Raheem, of Anastasia's secret meeting with the Prince in the orange grove. Therefore, through Raheem who knew Anastasia, there was still one other card she could play in case the men she had sent out failed to rescue Sanquo.

Raheem entered the room.

"You desire to know if the work is proceeding well?" he asked.

Gunara silenced him with her lean, claw-like hand upraised.

"Raheem, there are ill things toward—a shadow has passed over us. But the future of the Cause has been placed by Vishnu into the hands of you alone."

Raheem, little old harmless man, working for long years in his garden of roses, troubled and sad when blight came, or his roses bloomed too soon, now saw himself exalted strangely. The spark of fanaticism that had lurked in his simple old soul had been fanned to roaring flame by Gunara Tukaji. At their first meeting she had recognised his innocence, his simplicity, his faithfulness. Here was the material she sought, and with the unfailing eye of a ruler of men, she had picked him out for service.

"You, Raheem," she said, suddenly fixing him with her eyes, and allowing a gentle expression to cross her face, "you, Raheem, have little in strength, but much wisdom is yours. Therefore I need tell you nothing but that which you must do. Your own wisdom will give you all reason for that which I say. Therefore, Raheem, remember that the Cause is in thy hands!"

The old fellow clasped his gnarled hands together.

"Mother of men," he whispered, "what is it that I shall do?"

Gunara's face was inscrutable.

"At dawn you will go," she said, "to the young feringhee woman at the residency. She is to be take thence."

A swift, startled light leapt into the old gardener's eyes.

"No harm is threatened?"

"None," answered Gunara. "She will be safe in your hands.

But you must get her away at dawn, with a message that she is wanted urgently by the one whom she met in the orange grove. She will trust you, and will understand."

"Then, Raheem, you must take her to the Hidden House; she will be safe there, quite safe. There will be those there who wish to take care of her. By doing this little thing, Raheem, you will have served the Cause. You are wise, Raheem, and it is only you whom I can trust with this great work. Soon after dawn she must be taken away—" She paused for a moment. "You think, Raheem, that she will come easily, that she will not doubt you?"

"She will come easily," answered Raheem.

29

The Maharajah's Home-Coming

Harland stood in the House of the Silver Lily with Taylor's stained and bullet-riddled topee in his hand. His brows were contracted and his lips set in a thin line. Scarcely five minutes had elapsed since the helmet had been thrown in at the open window.

In those minutes a hundred surmises had passed through Harland's mind. At one moment he believed the helmet to be proof positive that Taylor was dead, at the next he thought it a ruse of one of Gunara Tukaji's emissaries evidently with the idea of drawing them back to the Temple. It was the Maharajah, however, who led them to a more satisfactory conclusion. He reminded them that Taylor was not wearing his topee when they left the underground stable of the gods. In his opinion the helmet had been seized, probably before Sanquo's men were routed, and had been flung through the window merely out of bravado. Harland's face lighted a little.

"Then you think Taylor may be all right?" he questioned.

"I think Taylor is well able to take care of himself," commented Carter.

"We owe our lives to Taylor," answered Harland, "and I should never forgive myself if anything happened to him. Suppose an attempt is made to rescue Sanquo before we get control in the Palace?"

"That," broke in the Maharajah, "is another reason, in my opinion, why we should go to the Palace at once. What do you think, Mr. Carter?"

"If you are ready I am ready," answered Carter brusquely. He drew out his watch. "We can get to the Palace by half-past three. Except the watchman, everyone will be asleep; if we don't pull things off successfully now, we never shall."

Five minutes later they were all three in the road, moving in the direction of the Maharajah's Palace. Seizing a favourable opportunity, when the guards were at the far end of the Palace, the three ran across the open space, towards the narrow door used only by the Maharajah.

Here for a moment there was an anxious pause. A year ago the Maharajah had had the door fitted with a combination lock, opening to the word "stealth"—what if that lock had been removed by Amoola Khan, or another word substituted?

The Prince stepped into the shelter of the doorway, and Harland and Carter stood, each looking in a different direction guarding against surprise. They had agreed to resort to strong measures if the guard surprised them. Scarcely a minute elapsed before the Maharajah drew a breath of relief, and the rattle of metal broke the intense silence.

The Maharajah touched Carter on the shoulder; his strong teeth gleamed in the moonlight; he held a brass lock in his hand.

A moment later the narrow door was opened on a void of inky darkness; the three men stepped into a passage scarcely wider than the door, which Carter carefully closed behind him.

They were within the Palace at last!

Carter could hardly repress his excitement. For the first time this secret method of restoring the Maharajah to his own struck him as bizarre and hazardous. He saw in a flash how much he and Harland had to lose, and how very little the British Government had risked. If any accident happened now at the last moment, the India Office would come upon the scene with an air of surprise and offended dignity, which would enable it to take a very strong attitude in the matter. Cater put a few whispered questions to the Maharajah; then, leaving him in the passage near the door, he and Harland, as had been arranged, felt their way forward until they came to a flight of steps. The walls on each side were so close as to brush their shoulders in the ascent.

They came at last to a little landing, and were confronted by a door, which Carter opened. Then, far away, along an endless Moorish corridor, Harland saw a dim light depending from the ceiling. The Maharajah had warned them that in this passage they might meet some of the guardians of the zenana. For some minutes they waited there with the door narrowly open, but no sound broke the stillness. They stepped into the corridor, and moved noiselessly and swiftly in the direction of the distant light, passing many doors on their right hand, and many windows, through which the moonlight streamed, on the left.

Arriving beneath the hanging light at last, they breathed, more freely. They were beyond the confines of the zenana, and on the threshold of the Palace proper.

The corridor still ran forward in the same direction, but was wider now, and was blocked by a number of tall, heavy screens, placed there to prevent anyone in the Palace obtaining a view of the corridor leading to the zenana. Carter had catechised the Maharajah so minutely that he appeared to know every inch of the ground.

They were within twenty yards of the door of the State bedroom, and Carter laid his fingers upon a bracelet in his pocket. The loan of this bracelet to Carter had been Kalim's last service to the Cause. Carter had asked for a showy bracelet, and Kalim had not failed him.

They passed the last screen, and nothing intervened between them and the corridor which Carter had inspected with Sanquo, except the coloured bead curtain, which hung across its whole width.

Noiselessly, step by step, and with infinite caution, they moved to the edge of this curtain, and peered through it. They were in darkness, but several shielded lights hung in the long, gorgeous corridor before them. They saw door after door to left and right; but it was the door of the State bedroom—the third door on the left—which held their gaze, and standing outside this door was a tall Pathan in uniform.

He stood motionless as the many armed gods in the Temple—he neither turned his head to left nor right. He might have been asleep, so still was he.

They watched him for a long time, then Carter drew the bracelet from his pocket. It was not easy to slide that bracelet towards the guard without disturbing the perfect silence which held the Palace in thrall. Minute followed minute, and Harland heard the ticking of his watch, and cursed himself for wearing it.

At length the silence was broken by a curious, low, droning sound, which issued from they knew not where. This sound continued monotonously and wearisomely. Then Carter suddenly clutched Harland's arm. There came a rapid slither of slippered feet behind them.

Someone was approaching from the zenana. On hands and knees they moved behind an angle of the nearest screen. Then a bent, white figure appeared, and moved forward through the bead curtain, and down the corridor.

They both knew that old, bent figure with its lithe, quick-moving head; they saw it pass the Pathan before the door of the State bedchamber, glance in his direction, and advance far down the corridor, until it turned in at a distant door.

After the passing of Gunara Tukaji, whose presence in the Palace had not surprised them, the Pathan seemed to relax his stiff attitude a little. He eased the belt about his waist with his thumb, moved his shoulders, and finally glanced about him.

That singular distant drone was still audible, and the Pathan, after a glance at the mosaic floor, suddenly squatted himself after the fashion, of his race. He was armed with a Snider and sword-bayonet, which he drew across his knees as he sat.

Carter and Harland had noiselessly returned to their old place, and were watching him through the bead curtain. They knew every inch of his contour now, though the shaded lamp hid his expression from them. At last Carter's hand stole through the curtain and laid the bracelet on the marble floor. Occasionally the Pathan stroked his chin. They saw his white eyeballs at length, as his eyes travelled over the screen—there was darkness behind that screen, and he knew nothing of their presence.

He was about to turn away again when his eyes focussed upon something which gleamed upon the floor. He looked away, and then back again, as if to assure himself that he had seen aright. A covetous light came into his eyes. At last, with a glance at the door behind him, he rose and moved with catlike softness towards the bracelet.

He bent to pick it up; then like a flash, a swift, strong hand grabbed him by the nape of the neck, and dragged him through the curtain. A handkerchief was thrust into his mouth, a man knelt on his chest. He believed the fiends of hell had risen and seized him, and were rending his soul from his body. He made a game resistance, but Carter and Harland were too many for him, and five minutes later he found himself propelled into a little room overlooking the Versailles fountain. A bright electric light burned above him, and before him stood a man in European garments, and this man was the Maharajah!

The covetous Pathan was sure of that—he had served the Maharajah all his life, and he was a man who knew His Highness when he saw him. And yet the Maharajah was drowsing on his old bed in the State room three doors off, for had he not heard the voice of his story-teller droning away scarcely five minutes ago, before he had been bewitched by that cursed bracelet.

It was only natural that it should take some minutes to convince this big, faithful fellow that he was not a victim of witchcraft—that Amoola Khan was an impostor, and that the real Maharajah had returned to claim his own. But he was convinced at length and he feel on his knees craving for pardon in that he had not instantly discovered and killed the impostor!

Carter and Harland stepped out of the room into the curtained corridor, leaving the Maharajah to remove any lingering doubts the Pathan might still have, and to swear him to secrecy for the future. They moved with less caution now, and presently halted before the gilt locked door of the State bedchamber. Amoola Khan, posing as the Maharajah, was in that room, and from within came a steady, droning, sing-song voice.

Carter turned the handle gently. As he had expected, the room was not locked, and the door opened smoothly and without noise.

Carter and Harland stepped quietly into the Royal bedchamber.

Lying on the Royal gold bed was Amoola Khan, his head sunk in deep pillows, his eyes half closed. Two feet away from the bedside, with his back to the door, squatted the story-teller—a queer Oriental figure in flowing robes.

There was a scent of Eastern spices in the air, oddly mingling with the distinct odour of jasmine flowers. For full fifty seconds after Carter and Harland's intrusion, the picture retained its tranquility—the story-teller still droned—Amoola Khan's eyes still drowsed.

Suddenly those eyes glared wide open. He raised himself from the pillows, remained transfixed for a moment, then sprang out of the bed with a yell of terror.

30

Daybreak

arland, leaping forward, swung his arm about Amoola Khan's waist, and swept him from the floor. For a moment he held the fellow thus—a ridiculous, struggling, frantic figure in cerise-coloured silk pyjamas. Harland spoke in his ear:

"If you don't stop that yelling—"

Amoola Khan understood, and grew quiet. He had recognised Harland at last—remembered him as the man he had met in the corridor of the Golden Pavilion Hotel, in London. In a flash, following that recognition, he knew that the game was up, and that his imposture was discovered. From the fellow's expression of countenance, it was clear that he expected nothing short of death at their hands.

"Amoola Khan," said Carter sharply, "you have been made a fool of! That unfortunate resemblance of yours to His Highness has been the ruin of you. Now, neither I nor Mr. Harland here wish you any particular harm." Amoola Khan's brown eyes travelled swiftly to Harland, and searched his face closely. "But," continued Carter, "we must know from your lips what Sanquo's game was—who was his confederates besides yourself and his mother." There was silence for a minute. "Are you willing to make a confession of all you know?"

Amoola Khan, grasping at the slender chance of exculpating himself, was more than willing to confess. He was quite clear-headed enough to know that unless Sanquo was a prisoner, these two men could never have penetrated to the State apartments. The game was clearly at an end, and his own skin was a now the only factor worth considering. The fright he had received had so unnerved him that he still trembled violently, and flinched at the slightest movement made by either Carter of Harland.

He told them the history of the conspiracy, as far as he knew it. He spoke in a low, even voice, which was almost a whisper, and he watched their faces narrowly for any sign of mercy towards himself.

He spun his story to a great length. Five—ten—fifteen minutes passed, and still the worlds flowed smoothly from his lips. There were facts embedded in the arabesque of his evasions, and Carter was quick to seize them.

Among the true things he learned from Amoola Khan's lips was the fact that it was Gunara Tukaji's printing presses, and Gunara Tukaji's ingenious brain, which had been sowing that part of India with seditious and inflammatory pamphlets.

"You say," interrupted Carter, "that this seditious paper is being printed in Kathnagar?"

"It is being printed in the Palace itself," answered Amoola Khan. "Gunara Tukaji had the machinery brought here in furniture-cases. No one suspected what was in the cases."

"But everyone in the Palace must know of the issuing of a paper from here?"

Amoola Khan shook his head.

"Her people are sworn to secrecy," he said, "they alone know of the work that is being carried on in the vaults of the Palace."

He was shivering as he spoke, and he sat on the edge of the bed, a pitiable object in his cerise-coloured pyjamas. The grand manner that he had assumed with such ease a few hour before in the Hall of Music had entirely left him; his attitude was abject. He was still wondering what was going to happen to him—whether or not he would escape from that terrible *impasse* with a whole skin—when the door of the bedchamber opened.

The Maharajah himself strode in; following him came the tall Pathan carrying his Snider!

Amoola Khan looked over his shoulder, and his eyes met the eyes of the Maharajah. The terror which he had shown in Harland's and Carter's presence was as nothing to the terror which now caused him to rise from the bed, and hurl himself full length on the carpet at the Maharajah's feet.

"Get up!" called the Prince harshly.

Amoola Khan rose to his feet. The Prince looked at him with eyes slightly narrowed. The resemblance between the two men was remarkable, but the indefinable air of hauteur and command, the regal dignity which had never left the Maharajah even in his darkest hours, marked the difference between them. Amoola Khan posturing as the Maharajah of Kathnagar was a mere actor playing a part; his real nature was timid and shrinking, and it had needed the iron hand and compulsion of Gunara Tukaji to enable him to dare what he had done.

The Maharajah was looking him over closely.

"Who are you?" he demanded.

"I am the son of Lallji, the dancing woman. I am of your blood; I am the lowest of your slaves. Truly, as I have stated, I am guiltless."

Carter and Harland suddenly heard the Prince break out into violent Hindoostani; his eyes blazed; the fact that this son of a dancing-girl had for a brief space stolen his own identity created a fury in him that caused amazement in the two men who had restored him to his rightful position. Harland was thinking to himself: "Well, he might have had the decency to thank us for what we have done; but, after all, perhaps it's natural to want to pour out his wrath on that miserable object."

Suddenly the Maharajah, who appeared to have forgotten the presence of Carter and Harland, made a sign to the Pathan behind him. The big fellow stepped forward and gripped Amoola Khan by the arm. A moment later the Pathan led his prisoner out of the room.

"What are you going to do with him?" asked Carter of the Prince the moment the door had closed on the two.

"I have not yet decided," answered the Prince. "For the present he will remain in safe keeping." He drew a deep breath. "So far," he said, "we have been very fortunate. I owe everything to you and to Mr. Harland."

"We're not out of the wood yet," answered Carter; "but I think we can assume that your Highness is once more Maharajah of Kathnagar."

Suddenly a knock came at the door of the room. The Maharajah cast a startled glance at Carter; then the door opened, and a servant of the Maharajah stepped into the room. The man repressed his surprise at sight of Carter, and salaamed low to the Prince.

"What does he say?" asked Carter, when the man had delivered a message to the Prince in Hindoostani.

"He brings a message," said the Prince, "summoning me to the room of Gunara Tukaji!"

"This is luck," said Carter, triumphantly.

The Prince glanced at the messenger.

"You may go," he said.

The man salaamed low, and withdrew; then the Maharajah turned to Carter.

"Gunara Tukaji—"he began. His face was stern. Carter broke into a laugh.

"Don't you see it?" he said. "It's the greatest piece of luck in the world. The old woman's simply put herself into our hands. She knows nothing of our coup to-night. In sending for your Highness she thinks she is sending for Amoola Khan—that is why her message is peremptory."

The Prince was thoughtful for a moment.

"I see," he said at length. "She has placed herself in our hands. She knows nothing. What shall we do?"

"Go to her," answered Carter, promptly. "I think when we have got the old lady we have gathered our net round the whole conspiracy!"

They passed out of the Royal bedchamber together; a bright light of excitement burnt in the Prince's eyes. Minute by minute the realisation that he was again Prince in Kathnagar was growing in intensity; the doubts and fears that had assailed his mind during the past weeks were slipping from him one by one.

He led Carter along the corridor, down a flight of steps, and towards the door of Gunara Tukaji's room.

"This moment was worth waiting for," whispered Carter as he went. "The old lady, has overreached as so easily and for so long a time that it will be the shock of her life to find she has fallen into our hands at least! Somehow I can't help feeling that when we inquire into matters we shall find that she is a far more important woman in the East than we had ever imagined."

"That is the room," whispered the Maharajah, raising a slim brown finger and pointing at a curtain in the distance. "It was formerly a room used by Krishna Coomar for the transaction of my business."

They reached the curtain, drew it back and stepped into the heavily-carpeted room, furnished with the board-table, Gunara Tukaji's desk, and the entirely Western clock which recorded the minutes on flicking squares of cardboard.

Gunara Tukaji herself was seated at the roll-top desk with her back towards them. Her mind was deeply occupied with the work before her. She head the door open, but did not look up or turn round.

"Come nearer!" she commanded.

Then she threw down her pen, leaned back in the swivel chair, and turned towards them. Carter was watching her with triumphant interest. For a second her eyes widened, and simultaneously her lean brown hands closed tightly. No other manifestation of astonishment or fear showed itself upon her keen brown features. It was Carter who broke the silence

"I think, my clever lady," he said, "we have got you at last."

Gunara Tukaji's eyes turned towards him; a peculiar expression of stupidity crept over her face, the expression that baffled Harland when he gripped her by the shoulder and charged her with entering the House of the Silver Lily. She opened her mouth to speak, but Carter was in no mood for subterfuge.

"Don't pretend you can't understand what I say," he said. "Your game is played out at last. You set for Amoola Khan, but it was not Amoola Khan who answered you summons!"

He turned and looked at the Prince. The Prince smiled; his eyes had been fixed steadily on Gunara's face.

"No," he said. "No, it was not Amoola Khan. Amoola Khan has already been imprisoned by me, and is awaiting his punishment. Your son also is awaiting punishment."

"What his Highness has said," commented Carter sharply, "is quite true. Your son was captured a few hours ago, and he was captured in the very act of attempting to assassinate His Highness; his case is a pretty serious one. As for Amoola Khan, the moment he fell into our hands he unburdened himself of everything he knew about you and your seditious conspiracy. The matter of the printing-presses for the dissemination of seditious literature was one of the first things he told us. Under the circumstances," he added finally, "don't you think it would be just as well if you'd drop your habitual cunning and chicanery, and acknowledge that the game is up?"

Gunara Tukaji was still for a further half-minute; then she rose slowly from her chair. A gleam of light took life in her keen eyes.

"But the game is not up," she said, in low, mellifluous tones; "far from it. So far as I am concerned, the game has only now begun."

"Oh, don't try that trick," said Carter, with an air of weary exasperation.

Gunara Tukaji glanced towards the Maharajah, and spoke again, still in excellent English.

"If Your Highness will allow me to seat myself again—I am no longer young—I will tell you how it comes that the game is still in my hands!"

31

Anastasia Receives a Message

On the morning following the Fête Anastasia's and Lady Strickley's trunks were packed, roped, and ready for the journey to Bombay. Sir Boris, fever-ridden and irritable, found himself lying awake cursing the day when Shooter Quilliam had seen fit to order his return to India. He was only half in the confidence of Carter and Harland, and he was quite oblivious of the doings in the vast crypt of the Temple of Vishnu. Anastasia, however, was waiting tremulously hopeful of news, and at dawn, when she stepped from her room on to the verandah and regarded the brilliant tumult of the garden with eyes of lingering affection, she was not surprised to see Raheem, the little old guardian of the rose-trees; she was not surprised to see him lift his bright eyes to her's, and then secretly beckon her to come down into the garden.

"Well," questioned Anastasia, "have you some new flowers to show me?"

"I bring you a message from one whose name I know not,"

said Raheem in a low voice. Despite the simplicity of his mind, he lied with perfect Eastern candour; the frank innocence of his eyes would have deceived even Gunara Tukaji. "I bring you this message," he went on, "that you are to come with me now, without delay. There is great reason for this haste."

"You bring no letter?" Anastasia's heart was beating rapidly; there was but one person in the world who would send her a secret message.

"I bring no letter," answered Raheem.

"Then how am I to know who this message is from?" smiled Anastasia.

"The mem-sahib knows," answered Raheem.

"And am I to come now?"

"An ox-cart is waiting near the gates of the garden," answered the old man. "The journey is not long, and the mem-sahib will be back before the others are astir."

He turned and began to move down the leafy avenue.

Anastasia followed him, believing, as Gunara Tukaji had foreseen, that none but the Maharajah had sent this message. The strange summons appealed to the romantic side of her nature, just as the meeting in the grove of orange-trees had appealed to her, and just as the splendour of the Maharajah, in his lilac tabard, his ropes of pearl, and his diamond aigrette, always filled her with visions of romance.

Near the gate of the garden a zebu-drawn, box-like vehicle was waiting at the roadside. Anastasia looked at her watch—save for herself, Raheem, and the driver of the cart the road was deserted—there were three hours to spare; she would not be missed for three hours, and, with a sensation of adventure, she bent low and stepped into the box-like vehicle.

Raheem walked at her side, and they talked as the strange cart trundled slowly along the red road.

At the end of an hour the vehicle stopped, and Anastasia alighted at the foot of a long, steep hill, with massive boulders of sun-baked rock, which incessantly diverted the narrow path of ascent into new directions.

Anastasia glanced about her, and noticed that some twenty yards away a palki was advancing, carried on the shoulders of six bearers. The long narrow box slung on bamboo poles, and with curtains drawn back, halted before her.

"They are from the one who sent me," explained Raheem, with a gesture towards the bearers. "They will take you to him. In the meantime I will await you here."

Anastasia hesitated for a moment, then stepped into the palki. An hour later, after a tortuous and steep ascent, which vastly exceeded the speed of the ox-cart, the palki journey also came to an end. Anastasia found herself in the small courtyard of a house, a courtyard of worn stone, with a dry fountain basin in the middle. There were movements behind the lattice-work at one side of the courtyard. Stray whispers came to her in the fresh morning air, and she was conscious that curious eyes were surveying her from behind the lattices.

For the first time a sensation of doubt entered her mind, then the thought of Raheem reassured her; he was waiting patiently at he bottom of the hill with his cart. She trusted Raheem; she knew that the old man would not permit himself to lead her into danger. The idea that Raheem, too, might have been deceived in the object of that journey never occurred to her mind.

The six bearers of the palki had withdrawn from the

courtyard; a heavy door closed behind them. A tinkle of metal sounded from the interior of the house, and a tall, handsome Native girl, wearing gold anklets, which clashed musically as her bare feet advanced over the timeworn stone, suddenly appeared. For a minute she and Anastasia eyed each other. Anastasia, admired the beauty of the stranger, the fine carriage of her head, the clear gaze of her superb Eastern eyes. She was conscious of an acceleration of her pulse, not created by fear of the woman, but by suspicion of the situation that appeared to be developing itself. The clang of the heavy door of the courtyard behind her had startled her from a romantic and trustful daydream.

The woman, who was of her own age, flung back the *sari* from her forehead with a graceful gesture of a bronze arm. Anastasia's feminine eyes detected the vanity of a movement designed to display luxuriant hair. The woman bowed, and speaking English with an attractive intonation, invited her into the house.

"Am I to wait there?" asked Anastasia, glancing about the room.

"If you please," said the handsome woman.

To Anastasia's surprise, she showed no signs of leaving the room, but with the utmost politeness entreated Anastasia to be seated.

Anastasia drew out her watch. Really, this was a little too much; nevertheless, she possessed herself in patience for a few minutes longer.

"Do you know why I have come here?" said Anastasia, at length.

The woman shook her head.

"I am to make you feel what you say 'at home'—entertain,"

she added, with a bright smile, "that is it I am to entertain.

Anastasia looked at her with a puzzled air, she was completely bewildered. A cold fear, like a hand of the suddenly gripped her heart, then almost simultaneously her self-possession returned. She turned indignantly upon the girl, and demanded to know why she had been brought to that house. But the girl had no information. Then, with an air of immense determination, Anastasia strode out of the little room and into the courtyard. The walls all round were high, the courtyard appeared to be deserted, but when she advanced to the heavy door which had closed behind her, she saw that it was guarded by a grey-bearded man, who leaned upon a staff of office, and who eyed her curiously as she approached.

Somehow she knew by the placidity of his expression, by a faint, triumphant gleam in his eyes, that the door was irrevocably locked upon her, that he possessed the key, and that no effort of her's could obtain it from him.

Why had she been tricked into coming to this place? She knew now of a certainty that Raheem had brought her a lying message.

Then she determined to tear the truth from the tall, handsome Native with the gold bangles. But here there was no satisfaction to be had; the girl knew neither why the mem-sahib was detained here, nor at whose orders she was detained.

During the remainder of that day, whereon she alternately raged with a fierce determination to get away and alternate despair, she met other members of the strange household—a large, pompous man, with an unusual puggari, three or four servants in snow-white costume, and from all of them she received deference and civility, and from none could she learn any reason for her captivity.

On the evening of the fifth night following her capture Anastasia stood at the window, looking out and upwards at the starlit night.

For many minutes she stood there, pondering on her amazing situation. Sometimes, as now, she felt inclined to believe the whole thing a dream. Anastasia was still at the window when the door curtains behind her were drawn softly aside, and a lithe, bronze-featured figure in a white *sari* slipped noiselessly into the room.

32

Gunara Tukaji Steals into a Room

"There's no doubt about it," remarked Carter, with irritation in his voice, "Gunara Takaji is still on top of the heap!"

"She's on the top of the heap," repeated Carter, speaking more to his boot-toes than to the Prince.

The Maharajah leaned back in his chair, and laid down the royal pen; he passed a slender brown hand over his forehead as he turned Carter.

"That is so," he said sententiously. "I had her before me again this morning," went on the Prince, "but there was no shaking her. Either I must give up Sanquo—" He paused a moment and hesitated.

"Or," interjected Carter, "Miss Strickley will never be seen in this life again—the old she-devil's determined on that point. And as your Highness has tried threats, bribes, and cajolery, everything in fact short of torture, it seems to me that the old woman has us!"

The Maharajah's lips closed tightly in a sudden hard line.

"My people," he said, "keep her under the closest observation. We are bound to win in the end; then the time of reckoning will come for this woman."

"So long as you keep a tight hold on Sanquo and Amoola Khan," resumed Carter, "we can go on searching for Miss Strickley; when we find her you can clap Gunara Tukaji into prison with her precious son."

Sometimes, when Carter discussed the situation which him, he saw a sombre light burn in the Prince's eyes, a light which boded ill for Gunara Tukaji, whose genius for evil had created this *impasse*.

Carter, who had been alone with the Maharajah during the whole of the morning, had noticed that, beneath all his apparent resolution, his determination was wavering. It was a hard thing to have to let go the captive Sanquo, the man who had attempted his assassination, who had accomplished the setting up of an impostor in his Palace, and yet there seemed no other way out of the difficulty. His love for Anastasia was gradually conquering his natural desire for vengeance.

Carter left the Prince, and on his way into Kathnagar that afternoon he called at the Residency, and shook hands with Taylor. Taylor, propped up on cushions, was lying on the verandah.

"Hallo!" he called, at sight of Carter. "What's the news?"

Carter shook his head.

"Things are pretty bad still," he said; "the old woman's still got us right enough."

"Have the Maharajah's people got hold of Hajiz yet?" inquired Taylor.

"No," said Carter. "Hajiz was the pleasant gentleman who threw your topee through the window. I owe him a particular grudge for that. It caused me to strew imaginary flowers on your grave!"

Taylor laughed.

"That was a cheap kind of mourning. I am sorry to disappoint you, but in three or four weeks, with the exception of a bit of a limp, I shall be as well as ever."

Carter moved towards the verandah, waved a hand at him, climbed into his saddle, and rode away. When he had gone a few hundred yards along the road a figure ran out from among the trees and salaamed before him. Carter drew rein. The man was a tall muscular fellow, and Carter recognised him as one of the Maharajah's servants. He spoke a little English.

"Is the Presence riding to the house of Gunara Tukaji?"

Carter told him that he was.

"Then," responded then man, "Mr. Harland Sahib said I must tell you this: *'The old bird has flown!'*"

Carter looked at him a minute.

"Hang on to my stirrup," he said at length, "and come along."

Ten minutes later he drew rein again before the house of Gunara Tukaji; the house that had been watched from every point of vantage by the Prince. Harland, who had been waiting, stepped out from Gunara Tukaji's garden.

"She's got away," he said. "How she did it Heaven alone knows!"

"She's bound to come back," said Carter. "Her whole scheme depends on making the Maharajah give in about Sanquo. She's got Miss Strickley sure enough, but the Maharajah's got her son."

33

A Face in a Mirror

Anastasia, staring dreamily out into the night, had not heard Gunara Tukaji step into the room, but suddenly there crept into her consciousness a sensation that she was not alone in the room, and with a sensation of dread she turned, looked over her shoulder and into Gunara's fathomless eyes. Instinctively the girl recoiled a step or two, but an ingratiating smile played over Gunara's hawk-like features.

"I am afraid I startled you," she said.

Anastasia noticed that her English was perfect, and without a trace of accent.

"You are Miss Strickley, are you not?" went on the old woman.

"Yes," answered Anastasia, doubtfully.

"Then I hope we may be friends," Gunara responded.

Anastasia's bows contracted. She wondered who the old singular-looking creature in the white *sari* could be; she wondered at her perfect English, her perfect ease of manner. Could it be that she was at last face to face with her real captor. She looked again into Gunara's features. There was something almost noble in that keen, dark visage.

"Can you tell me," asked Anastasia, "why I am a prisoner here?"

"I can tell you many things," said Gunara suavely.

"You can tell me?" repeated Anastasia.

"I can tell you. Moreover, I bring you a message from one who is waiting feverishly for news of you."

"You bring a letter?"

"A message."

Gunara Tukaji thrust her hand within the folds of her *sari*, and drew out a singular square case of lizard skin with a gold tassel. She asked Anastasia's permission to smoke, then from her case withdrew a thick cigarette. Anastasia handed her the matches, and she proceeded to smoke with a leisurely air.

"I bring a message," she went on, "from His Highness the Maharajah."

At the sudden mention of the Maharajah's name Anastasia felt the blood leap to her cheeks; her heart began to beat swiftly in wild relief.

"What is the message?" she asked breathlessly.

"He desire you to write to him."

"But his message?"

"That is his message."

Anastasia was puzzled.

"But if he knows where I am—" Then she stopped. It was enough for her that the Maharajah wished her to write to him; the very fact that he knew of her whereabouts was a proof of her safety, the desire for her to write was a proof of his love. She would write, of course she would write! The nerve strain of the last few days was forgotten in the passionate desire to communicate with the man she loved. She even for a while forgot her father and mother and the anxiety they must have suffered on her account.

"How will the letter be sent?" she questioned.

"I am in the service of His Highness," went on Gunara Tukaji. "He has entrusted me with the honour of his confidence in this matter. I will convey the letter."

"I can't write it at once, of course," said Anastasia, prettily confused. "I must have a little time to think; it will take me some time."

"His Highness needs just a short note—only a few words to tell him that he may meet you alone either early in the morning or at this hour to-morrow night at the foot of the hill where Raheem and his ox-cart left you."

"Oh," exclaimed Anastasia, "then I am to be released from this place!" Suddenly her brows lowered. "Why was I kept a prisoner here?"

Gunara Tukaji's serenity was undisturbed.

"His Highness will explain to you," she said. "He will explain everything. I am His Highness's servant, that is all."

The idea that she was to be free, that the Maharajah desired to meet her, swept every other thought from Anastasia's mind; and as Gunara Tukaji, crouching on the divan, tranquilly consumed her big cigarette, Anastasia drew a chair to the green-topped table and began the note she was to write. She found it impossible to confine herself to the bare statement Gunara Tukaji had suggested and her pen ran on almost of itself. The act of penning words to the Prince, to her prince, recalled his romantic image vividly to her mind.

She raised her eyes thoughtfully from the paper, and in a little oval mirror on the wall at her right, beyond the small lamp she caught the reflection of Gunara Tukaji's profile.

Gunara was not aware of her scrutiny, but suddenly Anastasia found her whole senses concentrated on that hard, keen outline, Until now she had regarded the woman who spoke such excellent English as a benevolent, elderly beldame, busily proud of possessing the Maharajah's confidence. Now she saw, immensely salient, an expression that was shudderingly cruel, that was menacing, watchful, and dangerous. Instinctively her eyes travelled from the reflection in the mirror to Gunara Tukaji's face, and Gunara smiled. But the evil that had been done; the suspicion that had been ignited in the girl's mind flamed to conviction. She sat back in her chair and looked squarely into the old woman's eyes.

"How do I know, she said, "that this message you bring me is a true one?"

Gunara Tukaji spread out her hands.

"What can it avail me," she said, "to bring a false message? If you do not desire to send word to His Highness, there is no need for such word; there is no more to say."

Anastasia rose from her chair.

"I do not trust you," she said, slowly and definitely. Then, after a minute's pause, she turned up the light of the lamp, took her letter, and held its corner over the flame of the chimney. As the letter crumbled and burnt, Gunara Tukaji laughed.

"You are very suspicious of an old woman!" She slipped from the divan and came to Anastasia's side. "Come, my dove, she said, in a voice of soft persuasion, 'write the letter. There is nothing to fear. You would not wish His Highness to think ill things of your? It is childish of you to doubt me. How could I know that you would desire to write to His Highness unless he himself had confided this secret to me?"

Anastasia flashed a glance at her. There was some truth in that. She hesitated a moment, and sat down at the table again, but the expression she had seen on Gunara's unwatched face had done its work. She recalled now for the first time that Gunara had practically dictated the terms of the letter she was to write. A fear that she was to be used as a decoy to lure the Maharajah into danger filled her with horror. She closed her fists firmly, her whole nature and spirit aflame with indignation.

"I will not write the letter!" she said, and as she spoke she rose and stood eye to eye with the formidable Gunara Tukaji. "I'll not write it, now or ever!" She drew in her breath quickly. "I believe that the whole thing is a trick and a lie!"

Gunara Tukaji, fighting for her son's life, knew that all the issues in the fight had been fined down to one—Sanquo's life depended on this letter being written. She had given up hope of breaking the Maharajah's resolution in any other way. Her capture of Anastasia had failed in the object she desired. There was only one chance left to her—she must again obtain possession of the Maharajah's person. She could do that now by a letter from Anastasia and in no other way. Sanquo's life, and possibly her own, hung on the writing of that letter. Therefore it must be written! The menace on her face, menace that could intimidate even Sanquo himself, caused Anastasia suddenly to quail her. But she clung to her resolution.

"I'll never write it!" she said. "Never, never!"

"You will write it now—to night!" said Gunara Tukaji, in tones scarcely louder than a whisper.

Anastasia backed away again. She realised at last that this sinister figure of vengeance was indeed her captor. The old smooth-voiced woman who had greeted her with florid politeness a few minutes earlier had utterly vanished. She felt a sickening dread and terror creeping in the elder woman's power and she listened as in a dream to Gunara Tukaji's slowly articulated words, demanding that she should re-seat herself at the table.

Suddenly she felt Gunara's claw-like grip upon her wrist, and, entirely against her own will, she found herself drawn and seated on the chair at the table.

She was conscious of a pen in her hand, of paper beneath her fingers. Then the spell snapped, and with a cry that was almost a scream, and with a sweep of her vigorous young arm, she sent Gunara Tukaji staggering and reeling into a corner of the room. The old woman flung out her arms and fell.

"I won't write!" called Anastasia, in a voice violent and intense, a voice shrill with hysteria. "I won't write!" She hurled away the pen. "I would rather die than write a word at your bidding!"

Her high voice appeared to echo and re-echo through the silent house. There was a pause; Gunara was gathering herself together. Running feet hurried through the passages to the door. Gunara Tukaji began to rise to her feet.

Anastasia stood before her, strangely altered, in rage and fury. In the girl's eyes was a ferocity that was half madness. Her gaze swept the room searching for a weapon, and Gunara Tukaji, for once in terror of her life, yelled for help at the top of her lungs.

Dark faces filled the doorway. Anastasia snatched the lamp from the table, and swung it above her head. Then powerful, clutching hands seized her.

Oblivion descended. ...

34

Raheem Speaks in Parables

"What's wrong with Raheem to-day?" asked Harland.

Taylor, who was seated on the verandah of the Residency, nursing his wound, turned his eyes towards the old gardener flitting about among his rose trees.

"I have noticed nothing," he said. "He was always an odd character."

Harland rose from his chair and, moving to the verandah edge, eyed the Native closely. He was unable to explain what it was that attracted his attention in Raheem's manner, but there was something distinctly unusual in the old fellow's movement. Of late Harland had been a passive on-looker in the tragedy that had overtaken the Residency, which had prostrated Lady Strickley, and which occupied the Maharajah's entire thoughts. Now, however, Raheem's movements filled him with a vague undefined hope; wordlessly the Native was conveying to him that something was in the wind.

Watching below the rim of his topee, he noticed that Raheem's eyes were fixed upon him from behind a distant rose-bush. Raheem's hands moved dexterously among the flowers, but Raheem's interest was, without doubt, centred upon the verandah.

"He's watching us," said Harland aloud. "He's been watching us for the last two hours. Now what's his game, I wonder?"

Taylor, whose only interest in life was that his leg should get better, thus fitting him for future "dust-ups" that would pale even the gorgeous fight in the Temple, said nothing. Harland, indifferent to Taylor's attitude, leaned over the verandah rail and beckoned Raheem towards him.

The old fellow hesitated a minute, then, emerging from his ambush of rose-trees, salaamed deeply.

"What is it, Raheem?"

Raheem raised his head, and looked into Harland's face—his dark, lined features were drawn in a tense expression, the bright old eyes moved fitfully. There was a look of apprehension in their liquid depths.

"What is it Raheem?"

"Nothing, Huzoor."

"You have been eyeing me for the last hour!"

Raheem bent forward and salaamed again.

"The Presence is mistaken," he said. "The roses on this side of the garden need much attention. The Presence has doubtless noticed that."

Harland smiled, and descended from the verandah.

"Now, Raheem," he said, with a note of authority, "tell me all about it!"

A startled light came into the old gardener's eyes. Harland noticed that his head wagged a little in the fashion of old people moved by excitement for held by fear.

"Raheem," he said, "I have been watching you. There was something you desired to say to Captain Taylor Sahib or to the Resident Sahib, and you were afraid. Then you thought of saying it to me."

"The Presence is mistaken," protested Raheem. He turned half away, in the attitude of one who awaits permission to go. "The Presence is mistaken," he repeated.

"You can trust me, Raheem."

"I would trust the Presence with my life," answered the gardener, looking into Harland's frank eyes. He spoke impulsively and quickly; then he turned away and glanced over the tree-tops beyond the confines of the garden. "There is nothing I have to impart," he said, clasping his hands together.

For a minute there was a vague light in his eyes, then he drew in his breath sharply. The struggle that had been taking place in his mind had come to and end, and when he spoke again he spoke in a low, steady whisper.

"I am afraid," he said, "for the safety of Miss Strickley sahib."

Harland felt his blood moved quickly, his heart begin to beat. He was surprised at his own emotion.

"I know nothing," said Raheem, in a voice that was almost a whisper; "but I have friends, perhaps more dangerous to me than enemies, and even that which I have said is unwise. If the Presence will promise me to forget—"

"I promise to forget."

"I know nothing," said Raheem in a dramatic monotone, "but if the Presence should desire to ride for his pleasure, he should take a strong horse, and ride from this garden, along the red road to the east. Half-an-hour's easy ride bring him to the foot of the Gupri Hill. Perhaps then the Presence would desire to mount that hill on his strong horse. The road is tortuous; there are many windings among the boulders smoothed by the wind and burned of the sun. Then at the journey's end, the Presence may be weary, but there are those who may give him welcome."

Suddenly Raheem stopped, and turned his keen, bright eyes, now steady and questioning, upon Harland's tense face.

"Does the Presence desire to take that ride?"

"If you mean what I think you mean," thought Harland, looking down at the old fellow's face, "I shall be astride that strong horse within the next ten minutes." Aloud he merely said: "I shall take the ride, Raheem."

A quarter of an hour later Harland, astride a superb Arab horse from the Residency stables, made his way out on the blood-red road, and, turning to the east, trotted smartly out of sight.

As he went, Raheem parted the bushes of his trees, muttered an invocation for his safety, and went back to his work. He was afraid; his old hands shook, and the figure of Gunara Tukaji, like a vast goddess of evil, lowered in his imagination.

The cause for which Raheem had been willing to lay down his life had required that Anastasia Strickley should be spirited away. He had submitted to Gunara Tukaji, believing her promise for Anastasia's safety. Innocently he had participated in that evil deed, but during the past two days there had travelled to him, in the strange fashion of the East, news of the doings in the Hidden House, visions of Gunara Tukaji's wrath, and visions of the young mem-sahib's courageous resistance. Then had begun a terrible struggle in the old man's mind. Miss Strickley sahib, white as the jasmine and beautiful as the dawn, had long since won Raheem's heart. And rather would he be torn to pieces than that evil should befall her. But still he was afraid; at thought of Gunara Tukaji his heart melted within him. So it came that, after the oblique fashion of his race, he imparted the secret of Anastasia's hiding-place in the form of a parable.

Fortunately, he had chosen Harland instead of Taylor. Harland was quick to understand the meaning of that parable, and, despite the fact that the hour was not one for exertion, he pressed his horse eagerly forward beneath the almost vertical rays of the sun.

"Harland," he said to himself, "if life is to be saved you must save it. What is to be done must be done single-handed. It must be done now!"

He came at length to the foot of the hillside. Vast boulders baking in the brazen sunshine hid the tortuous path of ascent.

Harland dismounted and mopped his brow; the enchanted somnolence of mid-noon dominated the scene. No one was within sight; the harsh cry of paraquets in a distant grove came to him faintly. Still further away, in the direction of the city of Kathnagar, a well-wheel creaked uneasily.

He raised his eyes to the sun-baked hillside. For a thousand feet or so above him the narrow path wound among immense boulders. The place looked utterly barren and desolate.

Harland patted his horse's neck.

"Come, old lady," he said, "we'll walk up together." And together they made the ascent.

For more than two hours they continued the upward

journey, pausing incessantly, and upon Harland's part making a cautious survey of every new stretch of path which revealed itself. At the end of an hour horse and rider came upon a small coppice of shrivelled trees. Here Harland called a halt, and, finding a shady place tethered his horse and continued his investigations alone. He had followed Raheem's directions minutely, and suddenly he stepped from beyond the coppice and looked up the further hillside. Above, surmounting the brow of the hill, a long, low wall, broken and crumbling, and with trees forcing apart the heavy stones of its surface, ran athwart the sky line. Harland had never seen anything more desolate than that long, sun-baked wall crumbling to dust. For some minutes he remained motionless, regarding the wall which marked the southern front of an ancient city, long since forgotten and fallen into decay.

Harland stepped out into the blazing sunshine, crossed a small plateau, and mounting the steep hillside reached the foot of the wall. Using tree-trunks and age-old crevices, he ascended easily to its summit, and looked down upon this strange city of the dead. Gnarled and twisted trees rose from the sand-buried ruins, but there was no sign of human life. Harland descended and walked ankle-deep in the red, sun-heated sand. He was thinking of Raheem and of Anastasia Strikcley. The old gardener had meant him to come here, there was no doubt of that, but, so far as he could see, there was no possibility of a hiding-place.

The thought that perhaps, after, all he had been led a wild-goose chase occurred to him and filled him with anger. He had hoped for a discovery of some kind, and nothing but the utmost desolation and dreariness had met him. He sat down on a low wall to think, and fifty feet away something grey and hairy

moved among the ruins. Harland slipped behind the wall, swift
as a lizard, then laughed to himself. The beard he had seen was
the beard of a goat, which continued to move slowly across his
line of vision. For some minutes he watched the animal make
its way among the ruins and noticed that it headed languidly in
one direction. Presently the clear air was penetrated by a low
distant cry. The goat cocked its ears and broke into a run.

In a flash Harland followed, leaping over rubble and dashing
through broken walls as he went. Suddenly the goat ascended
a short slope, and appeared to vanish into a smooth, long wall.
Harland waited for some minutes, then he, too, ascended the
slope and inspected the wall.

The house referred to by Gunara Tukaji as the Hidden
House lay within the square, sun-baked quadrangle. The goat
which had disappeared, had entered by a heavy, iron-barred
door, with a grille the height of a man's eyes.

Harland, whose mind was working with unusual rapidity,
withdrew to the shelter of a pile of stones.

"Raheem meant well after all; she's in there, behind that
high wall," he said to himself. "No one would ever think of
searching in such a place as this." He paused and pondered the
situation, eyeing the high, sun-baked wall that surrounded this
house of the living in a city of the dead. "Now," he thought,
"shall I go down and acquaint Sir Boris and the Maharajah, or
shall I see what I can do by myself?"

Then the idea of a saving Anastasia Strickley without aid
took possession of his brain. The something that had revealed
itself out of the depths of his heart told him that not even a
moment must be lost. If Anastasia were behind those frowning
walls he must get to her, he alone, not the Maharajah, not Taylor,

not Carter. The door—the fine old black door with the grille—was impregnable, but the wall was not unscalable. If he could get to the top of the wall without being disturbed, he might look down into the courtyard and take accurate bearings of the house.

In following the goat he had exhibited a certain amount of strategical skill; he must continue to act in the same manner, and there was no knowing what might be the result. He emerged from the shelter of his pile of stones, and made a detour of the four high walls surrounding the Hidden House. Having satisfied himself that there was but one entrance—that of the black door with the grille the height of a man's eye—he set to work to find an easy place to scale.

35

The Whispering House

Five minutes later Harland was lying full length on the burning summit of the wall. Whatever his limitations might be he was an excellent hunter. The chase in any form appeared to stimulate him to a surprising keenness and ingenuity. Therefore he refrained from peeping into the courtyard below. A single mistake, a single false move, and the hoped-for plan of a single-handed rescue would vanish. Therefore he succeeded in restraining his eagerness. And at last he made his cautious way down from the wall, through the ruined city, and again sought his horse tethered below the plateau. He had thought out his plan of campaign, and he needed a rope. A long knotted rope was essential to his success.

When next he drew near to the wall of the Hidden House, both horse and man had been duly refreshed; night had fallen, the vast amphitheatre of the sky was silvered with stars, and Harland, giving his horse a whispered word of encouragement and comfort, scaled the wall of the Hidden House as silently and as dexterously as he had scaled it in the light of day. For the second time he found himself lying face downward on the summit of the wall; this time caution was not so necessary. He drew himself, snake-like, to the edge of the wall, and peered cautiously into the fascinating courtyard.

Below him was the basin of a dry fountain with a timeworn balustrade. To the right under the archway, he made out the murky figure of the guardian of the door, and old, bearded man whose features were indistinguishable in the darkness. Save for the door-keeper, the courtyard below him was entirely deserted, but from a ground-floor window of the house, a window over which a rush curtain was drawn, a faint haze of light made itself visible. He had already made use of this long, knotted rope, which now hung down the inner side of the wall.

With infinite stealth, Harland at last launched himself over the inner edge of the wall, and dropped noiselessly upon the top rail of a verandah. If at that moment he had slipped, or had created more than a minimum of sound, his adventure would have reached its climax—Anastasia Strickley's hiding-place would have remained unknown; Gunara Tukaji would have still triumphed.

Many breathless minutes followed before Harland, balancing himself with one hand against the sun-baked wall, dared to descend from his perch; then he lowered himself to the verandah, and on hands and knees crept towards the lighted window—and disappointment, for he could neither see nor hear anything.

Now, what was going on in that lighted room? Was Anastasia Strickley there—or Gunara Tukaji, who had so mysteriously vanished from Kathnagar—or was the room empty?

He craned his neck in an attempt to obtain a view of the interior. It was distinctly unusual that a window should be concealed in that fashion. He decided to desert the window, and seek the door of the house itself. And a minute later he was moving softly forward through an open doorway into darkness.

The house was an old one, built in two storeys, and suddenly, as Harland groped with extended arms in the darkness, a flare of light a little further along the passage startled him, and caused him to flatten himself against the wall.

The door-curtain of a room had been drawn back, and in the aperture stood a tall Native girl. She carried a small lamp in her hand, and if her eyes had swept the passage she would have seen Harland.

As it was she turned and made her way into the interior of the house. Harland began to realise that matters were slipping out of his hands, that the work before him was far more complicated than he had foreseen. His position in the passage was entirely untenable; at any moment one or other of the inhabitants of the house might come upon him. Even now he heard voices in the distance, and above him the soft patter of footsteps. A light was moving in the upper storey of the building casting flickering reflections on the ancient staircase. A moment later Harland was outside the house.

A few minutes later Harland again slipped inside the house, and this time the curtain over the front-room doorway had not been fully drawn.

Harland placed his fingers gently upon the curtain edge and widened the aperture. At the far side of the room on a divan, and with her face upturned, a face that was white, drawn, and fear-haunted, sat Anastasia Strickley!

Anastasia was looking at a woman whose features were hidden from Harland—a short woman in a white *sari*, who stood immovable. Neither woman spoke, and Harland, who could hear whispering voices in other parts of the house, stared in bewilderment. What was taking place?

Harland through the narrow aperture between the curtains and the door, saw Gunara's face—he had never seen anything quite like that face in his life. A sudden, swift instinct to step into the room and place his hands round the lean old neck swept over him. For a fraction of time nothing would have given him greater pleasure than to have choked the life out of those swift-moving, diabolical eyes.

Gunara Tukaji's fist smote the table sharply, her head flashed round in Anastasia's direction.

"You will write the letter!"

Anastasia drew in a deep, shuddering breath, covered her face with her hands for a moment, and, still with her hands covering her face, shook her head slowly.

Then Harland stepped quite noiselessly into the room. In a flash he gripped Gunara Tukaji's right wrist with a power that threatened to crush the bones. He knew his antagonist, and the barrel of his Mauser was within a foot of her head.

He had never in his life felt careless of a human existence until that moment.

"You old she-devil!" he whispered between his teeth.

"If you open your mouth or utter a sound, I'll pull the trigger, and thank God for giving me the chance! Now sit over there!"

He motioned her to the inner corner of the room, releasing his grip on her wrist, but never for an instant uncovering her with the revolver. Gunara Tukaji's power of simulating extreme stupidity puzzled him—the woman he had seen through the curtains and the woman who now looked up at him were entirely different persons. But she was Sanquo's mother, Harland remembered that, and tactics of this kind had little effect on his mind; all he knew was that he was in the presence of the most dangerous criminal east of Suez. Inevitably he would have pulled the trigger if Gunara Tukaji had made the faintest motion towards escape. Perhaps the old woman was fully conscious of the danger in which she stood, for she crouched down in the corner, and held up her hands as one to whom firearms are strange, uncertain weapons.

Anastasia Strickley had risen from the divan like a ghost. Harland glanced at her for a moment, and whispered:

"Miss Strickley, I've come to take you away!"

The girl nodded weakly, as though in a dream.

"Thank God," she whispered—"Oh! Thank God! Thank God!"

"If you have the courage," Harland went on, "to slip out of here while I keep this fiend, you can get away. If you go to the end of the verandah"—Harland pointed with his hand—"you will find a knotted rope hanging there. Use it to pull yourself up to the top of the wall—I have made the rope secure."

His eyes were on Anastasia, as he spoke, but his pistol still covered Gunara Tukaji, crouching in her corner. Suddenly a metallic crash sounded through the room, a heavy bronze tray fell rattling to the floor, sending gong-like echoes through the quiet house.

Harland flung a glance at Gunara Tukaji, but she was still crouching motionless in her corner. Nevertheless he knew that, during the fraction of time which his eyes had not been upon her, she had jerked the floor-mat with her foot and brought down the tray.

"Go! Go!" he called suddenly to Anastasia; "I'll guard the door of the house."

He reached out swiftly, and seizing the girl by the arm dragged her forward; a minute later she was outside the house and on the dark verandah.

Harland set himself upon the doorstep of the Hidden House.

Footfalls, which began to approach with the crashing descent of the tray, now advanced at a run as Gunara Tukaji's voice, screaming in Hindoostani, suddenly rent the air.

Harland expected that she would call out when he left the room with Anastasia, and he was prepared for what happened. A large fat man, holding a lamp, came plunging along from the depths of the house. He halted and hesitated at seeing Harland in the doorway. In the meantime, Anastasia had made her way to the wall, and was groping about for the rope Harland had spoken of.

The fat man fell back and retired stealthily for a weapon, and Gunara Tukaji, in the front room, fell unexpectedly silent. Harland became anxious—without doubt she was up to devilry of some sort. A rending sound came to him. He glanced over his shoulder and saw that Gunara Tujaki had wrenched away the rush window curtain, and was stepping out of the window on to the verandah. She paused a moment with hands fumbling in her *sari*, then advanced upon Miss Strickley, whose back was towards her. Harland saw Anastasia ascend nimbly to the rail of the verandah; she had found the rope and was about to pull herself up to the summit of the wall, when something flashed in Gunara's hand.

Harland fired. It was all he could do, there was nothing for it but to fire, and for a moment he saw Anastasia's startled face turned towards him; then as the echoes of his shot died away, he heard Gunara Tukaji's knife clink to the matted verandah, he heard the old woman scream and saw her lean for support against the balcony rail. Then his heart gave a leap, Anastasia had again turned her attention to the rope. She was swarming up it, her hand was already on the top of the wall.

A moment later she had drawn herself to comparative safety.

The interior of the house had grown strangely silent.

Gunara Tukaji, leaning wounded against the black wall, the old doorkeeper flitting uneasily about, and Harland himself striving to keep an eye on four places at once, appeared to be the only occupants of the scene.

Presently Harland's ear detected new sounds in the interior of the building—a shot whistled along the passage through the dark doorway, and into the courtyard; a second shot followed.

Harland put his wrist round the edge of the doorway, and fired twice into the interior of the house, then leaping into the courtyard, made to run along towards the wall. As his feet touched the flagstones a writhing figure leapt upon him. The old doorkeeper was making frantic attempts to cut into him with a knife. The man's strength was little more than that of a child, and Harland whisked the weapon from his lean hand, tapped him deftly on the head with his Mauser, and made for the rope. He was on the rail of the verandah when Gunara's voice again shrilled out into the darkness. She was calling her men from the interior of the house, exhorting them to courage.

"Come out, ye cowards! Come out, cowards!—Cowards!" she screamed.

Apart from her shrill rage there was a note of pain in her voice, and Harland noticed that she hugged her arm tightly. In the interests of good government it was probably his duty to terminate her seditious existence, but good government counted little with him then. He leapt towards, the hanging rope and grasped it, and as he did so he glanced back at the house and saw a large globular head obtrude itself from the doorway.

For a moment he hesitated. That pumpkin-like head was an alluring mark, but there was Miss Strickley to think of, and promiscuous shooting was not his *rôle* for the moment.

With a final heave he drew himself up to the broad flat summit of the wall. Miss Strickley was there, crouching away from the tumultuous courtyard. She was exhausted and terrified, and the crash of rifle shot from a man in the doorway did nothing to steady her. Gunara Tukaji's high voice yelling in Hindoostani still assailed the night; other voices joined the tumult, and Harland seized Anastasia *sans* ceremony about the waist.

"There will be the devil to pay in a minute," he whispered. "Slide down this rope!"

He swung her to the outer edge of the wall, held her as long as he could, and a minute later followed, letting himself drop into ankle-deep sand beyond the wall.

In the starlight he glanced at her pallid, tense face.

"Now," he said, in a low voice, "we must make a bolt for it!"

And with lowered heads they ran zigzaging among the ruins of the dead and forgotten city. Yielding sand silenced their footfalls.

An hour later, when Harland lifted Anastasia to the saddle of his horse, her eyes shone in the starlight, and she leaned a little towards him.

"Thank you, dear Mr. Harland," she murmured breathlessly. And Harland, smiling, slipped his arm through the bridle and set out upon the blood-red road to Kathnagar.

36

Conclusion

Harland had returned to England. Eight months of India's suns had browned his skin; he was lean, active, and lithe as a cat, and as he sat at a table with a pen in his hands, the pallid English sun penetrated the window of his office.

Harland's eye drifted from the paper before him and dwelt dreamily upon the beam of light. Memories of the busiest months of his life pictured themselves in his mind, and flinging down the pen he rested his forehead on his hand.

"I can never do it," he bewailed inwardly; "legs under a desk, and shoving a pen from morning till night!" Sanquo's face rose before him, the reeking Temple of the Gods, the Hidden House—then a picture of lustrous black hair, of clear grey eyes, of a skin white as jasmine, and of a ride through the night along the blood-red road to Kathnagar drove out every other memory.

He sat up in his chair, and again seized his pen.

"Harland!"

He turned swiftly towards the door. Dacent Smith, that supreme product of an easeful civilisation, was regarding him with pleasant cynicism. Dacent smith, exorbitantly bald, sleek, and with his monocle twinkling as ever, crossed the floor and laid a hand upon his junior's shoulder.

"Shooter Quilliam's coming to see you."

"When?"

"Now! He likes your report of the Kathnagar business."

"Curse reports!" said Harland, briefly.

And as he spoke heavy pounding footsteps were heard in the corridor outside, the door was thrust open, and Shooter Quilliam stepped into the room.

"Harland," he said, in his sift, high-pitched voice, "I like your report." He ploughed his way across the room and gripped Harland's hand. "I like it," he repeated, and turned his full heavy-lipped face forwards Dacent Smith.

"It is very gratifying to me that you like it," responded Harland, with the politeness due from himself to the Secretary of State for India.

"A most valuable piece of work," responded Shooter Quilliam, generously; "I am glad the Maharajah of Kathnagar appreciated what you and Carter did!"

"It was very kind of you to allow me to keep his presents, sir," responded Harland.

"I did nothing of the kind!" pealed Shooter Quilliam, with a glance at Dacent Smith.

"Of course not," said Dacent Smith; "such a thing would be entirely without precedent!"

He turned and winked at a steel engraving of Clive over the mantelshelf.

Shooter Quiliam permitted Harland to be seated, and took a chair himself; Dacent Smith stood at the window and alternately glanced into St. James's Park and polished his monocle.

"There is no unrest whatever in Kathnagar?" observed Shooter Quilliam.

"None whatever," Harland answered.

"It is a pity Gunara Tukaji, slipped through your fingers!"

"It is entirely my fault, sir," answered Harland, candidly. "I might have—have removed her, but in doing so I might have failed to rescue Miss Strickley."

"Of course—of course."

There was a note of irritation in Shooter Quilliam's voice. He paused a moment, drumming with his fingers upon the desk.

"In the months you were in Kathnagar following the Maharajah's restoration you heard no word of her?"

"She vanished utterly," answered Harland, "and at the present moment is no doubt fomenting discord and sedition like one o'clock. Our only satisfaction is that she can't live for ever!" He paused a moment, then went on, "She is an amazing woman, sir. As I said in the report, when her son Sanquo was condemned in the Maharajah's Court to ten years' penal servitude, an emissary of his mother's flung him a screw of paper, which he caught deftly. He swallowed the paper's contents, and died before he could be removed from the dock. The paper," said Harland reminiscently, "contained a tabloid of cyanide of potassium and a message from his mother."

"What a woman!" ejaculated Shooter Quilliam in admiration. He put his hand in his breast pocket, drew out a thick morocco-covered notebook, and opening it carefully, removed a small square of rice-paper, with two faintly pencilled, lines in Hindoostani upon it. After looking at the paper thoughtfully for a minute, he handed it to Dacent Smith.

"Translate it, Smith," he commanded.

And Dacent Smith holding the fragile paper in his hand, read aloud:

"A present from Gunara Tukaji to her son, who proved himself too small for a great enterprise."

A memory of the reeking Court House in Kathnagar, of Sanquo flashing his hand to his mouth, and almost immediately writhing to the floor of the dock, leapt through Harland's mind.

"Handle the paper gently," said Shooter Quilliam. "I intend to keep it as my memento of a very pretty business." When he had again enclosed Gunara's last message to her son within the leaves of his pocket-look, he turned to Harland once more.

"In your report," he said in his incisive, sharp voice, "you omit all mention of a particular fact."

Harland glanced at him enquiringly.

"The little love affair between the Maharajah and Sir Boris Strickley's daughter," explained Shooter Quilliam.

Harland moved uncomfortably.

"There was nothing in it," he said, "a girlish romance, Miss Strickley was very young sir."

Dacent Smith moved quickly from his window.

"Sort of thing," he interposed, "that often happens in India. Handsome Native Prince—beautiful English girl—young, romantic—"

Shooter Quilliam glowered at him.

"Harland has the facts," he said curtly.

But Harland's *savoir faire* had entirely deserted him. He

fingered his necktie uneasily and glanced at Dacent Smith.

"She is now engaged," ventured Dacent Smith, "to an English gentleman."

A flicker of surprise came into Shooter Quilliam's small eyes.

"If I remember aright," he said, "she was deuced pretty girl."

"A very beautiful girl," said Dacent Smith. He looked significantly at Harland, who gave a final pull at his necktie and decided to face it.

"We are going to be married in October, sir," he confessed with clumsy abruptness.

On a certain October night the Maharajah walked solitary in an orange grove of Kathnagar. A little night wind stirred—white orange petals, detaching themselves from the trees, floated earthward.

The Maharajah halted in his walk and held out a slender hand to the falling blossoms.

"Rao, the petals are falling,'" he murmured in his empty heart; and turning, retraced his steps towards the glittering windows of his Palace.